"Are you nervous?" Kip asked Bear as the car carried them through the dark Manhattan night.

"No. Yes. I don't know, I have to think about it," he muttered without meeting her eyes.

"Maybe I should have stayed home," she said sharply. "You'd be in a better frame of mind."

Startled, Bear turned to look at her. For a long moment they stared at each other. The air seemed to vibrate with suppressed desire. As if unable to stop herself, Kip leaned toward him. His gaze flicked to her lips. Then he gathered her into his arms, his mouth coming down on hers in a warm, searching kiss.

Surprise rendered her limp for a moment. Then she struggled to be free. An instant later, though, she didn't want to be free, and that knowledge shocked her more than the kiss. . . .

WHAT ARE *LOVESWEPT* ROMANCES?

They are stories of true romance and touching emotion. We believe those two very important ingredients are constants in our highly sensual and very believable stories in the *LOVESWEPT* line. Our goal is to give you, the reader, stories of consistently high quality that may sometimes make you laugh, sometimes make you cry, but are always fresh and creative and contain many delightful surprises within their pages.

Most romance fans read an enormous number of books. Those they truly love, they keep. Others may be traded with friends and soon forgotten. We hope that each *LOVESWEPT* romance will be a treasure—a "keeper." We will always try to publish

LOVE STORIES YOU'LL NEVER FORGET
BY AUTHORS YOU'LL ALWAYS REMEMBER

The Editors

LOVESWEPT® • 396

Helen Mittermeyer
Men of Ice:
Black Frost

BANTAM BOOKS
NEW YORK • TORONTO • LONDON • SYDNEY • AUCKLAND

One

Spring was struggling to overtake winter, and a watery sun was trying to beam. There was frost in the air and in the man who approached the racing car. Frost was natural for March in Michigan. For the man, it had taken years of risking his life, and of once coming too close to death, to acquire his icy patina.

Beryl Kenmore, called Bear by everyone, didn't want to be at the isolated track outside Detroit. His one-time mechanic and long-time friend Gunder Bailey had talked him into flying to Michigan to see the test drive of a new revolutionary car.

Marketing such a machine could be exorbitantly expensive. His company, Kenmore Motors, had taken chances when it came to the unusual, but Bear had never been foolhardy.

Several people were milling around the race track, and Bear recognized owners and engineers from other car companies. Preferring not to socialize, he started toward the car when a musical laugh made him turn his head.

Standing beside the owner of a Japanese car company was a tall blond woman. She was beautiful . . . and more. The sunlight caught the golden hair streaked with platinum and turned it to precious fire. Bear had seen many attractive women in his time, young and old, dark and fair, but the blonde was magic. Sexy, too. Her long legs were curved with muscles. Somehow she appeared both strong and dainty.

Changing his direction so that he could intercept her, he heard her tell the other man that she had to go to the office but would be back shortly. She stepped into a car and drove away, leaving Bear feeling a strange sadness, as though he'd just lost something valuable. He couldn't explain the sudden dry ice feeling inside himself, or why the blonde had had such a potent effect on him. Women had always been a part of his life. He liked it that way. Why had this particular woman sent such stinging arrows of excitement sweeping through him?

Pushing the beautiful woman totally from his mind was impossible, but he resumed his course toward the car nonetheless.

The racer looked like a sleek shark with wheels, glinting diamond black in the sun.

"So what'ya think, Bear?" Gunder asked. "Great, huh?"

Bear nodded. "Looks good."

He studied the car's aerodynamic lines, remembering the stats he'd read on it when he'd been invited to the test drive. If the car lived up to all the expectations of its designer, Phineas Noble, it would be a magnificent machine. It was too bad Phineas had died before his prototype was finished.

Bear's gaze swept over the car. He could almost hear the roar of its motor, though the car was silent, dark, lethal. It was a beauty. If he'd still been driving, he might have tried to buy it for himself.

As though the memories of his racing days mesmerized him, he put his hand on the door handle.

"Bear," Gunder said quickly. "The owner doesn't want you to touch it." The wiry man pointed at the DO NOT TOUCH sign.

"Is that right?" Bear said softly.

"Hey!"

Bear turned at Gunder's surprised exclamation, but too late. A woman shoved him back from the car. He fought to keep his balance, grabbing the woman's arm. As she tried to free herself, he lost the fight and fell to the ground, the woman landing on top of him.

"What the hell . . . ?" he muttered. Tendrils of gold hair touched his face, and he inhaled a very special essence, enhanced by a hint of Chanel No. 5.

"It says do not touch," the woman said, pointing to the sign next to the car, as Gunder had.

The blonde was back! Bear thought. And more beautiful close up than at a distance. He knew who she was now. Kirsten Patricia Noble, Phineas Noble's niece and owner of the "black shark" car. Lissome and curvaceous, she had alluring aqua eyes and luxurious hair, coiled on top of her head, streaked with gold and platinum. What would it be like to have its heaviness covering his face? he wondered. Unconsciously he lifted his hands to grasp her small waist, pulling her closer so he could study her face.

She stiffened instantly. "Let me go, Mr. Kenmore."

Kip knew who he was. She hadn't expected him to be so big, though. With midnight-blue eyes and coal-black hair, he was a masculine powerhouse. Angry and embarrassed as she saw people gathering around them, she tried to push herself off him.

His grip tightened, and he grinned. "Uncomfortable?"

"I'd like to get up," she said tautly.

Once again she attempted to free herself. His eyes closed as her lower body pressed against his.

"You're a beautiful lady, Kirsten Patricia Noble," he whispered.

"And you're a clod." Kip rolled to one side and off him, pretending not to hear the sexual hiss of his breath when her hips again seemed to mold to his.

Clambering to her feet, she glared down at him. "That car is mine. Don't touch it again."

Bear rose slowly, brushing at his clothes. "Valkyrie," he murmured. "A very slender one, but still a warrior lady."

Kip brought up her closed fist. "Enough of one to deal with you, fella."

"Oh, I'm sure of that."

She was jolted by his sudden smile. He had dimples. Incredible. Her chin came up. "I'm not into double entendre."

His smile broadened. "I see."

Why did she feel she was walking on quicksand, as though she'd just been threatened? she wondered. "Now, about the car—"

"Who's test driving it today?" he interrupted.

"I am."

"What?"

Disconcerting him gave her great satisfaction. "Did that throw you off stride, Mr. Kenmore?"

"No, you did that a few moments ago."

She turned and started walking away from him. "Watch yourself. I might do it again," she said over her shoulder.

"Feel free," he answered silkily.

"Hey, Bear," Gunder muttered to him. "What's going on? I thought you didn't know Miss Noble."

"I do now."

"What's that mean?"

Bear turned to look at his friend. "Nothing. I just found something very valuable."

"The car?" Gunder asked eagerly.

"The woman," Bear said, his gaze glued to Kirsten Patricia Noble as she pulled on a cream-colored driving suit. She tucked the helmet and gloves under her arm and strolled to the car.

"Get me a suit, Gunder. You know the size." Bear headed toward the car, stopping to pick up a helmet and gloves as Kip climbed into the driver's seat.

"Didn't you hear her?" Gunder muttered as he thrust a suit at him. "Her car—"

"I know." Bear pulled on the one-piece suit. "That track ice free?"

"Guess so." Gunder ran a practiced gaze over the tarmac oval. "Looks hard and fast." His eyes narrowed. "Maybe tricky in spots."

"That's what I figure." Moving quickly, Bear strode around the front of the car and climbed into the passenger side.

"Get out." Kip tightened her grip on the wheel to keep her hands from shaking. Bear Kenmore had taken all the oxygen in the car. Damn him! She didn't want him critiquing her driving.

"No," he said. "You drive. I watch." He strapped on his seat belt. "Fire the damn thing, Kirsten Patricia Noble."

Even in the bulky suit she looked gorgeous, he thought, unable to stop staring at her. The woman had power. And she was smart. His memory had kicked in, and he remembered reading an article about her after her uncle had died a year ago. She had a master's degree in business from the Maxwell School at Syracuse University, and her uncle had grounded her in each of his various business interests. On his death, she'd assumed command of all of those interests, and was starting to put her own stamp on things. The article had stated she enjoyed best working at the textile company her uncle owned. The article had neglected to mention how beautiful she was.

"I'm called Kip," she said through her teeth.

"Unclench your jaw and get out there."

"Don't dictate to me."

"You're as tough as your uncle," Bear said, chuckling.

"My uncle was a wonderful man and a genius," she said tightly.

"But tough."

A reluctant smile touched her mouth. "Yes."

She fired the engine. It roared to life, and Kip maneuvered across the verge and side area toward the flat track.

Why had Honey Bear Kendall suddenly appeared at the track? she wondered. After she'd sent the invitation to the test drive, she'd received a terse note from him stating he probably wouldn't be there. What did he want? He didn't race anymore.

Her hands were suddenly moist in the driving gloves, and she tightened her grip on the wheel. Dammit! Why was she nervous? She'd teethed on socket wrenches and had been driving for years.

The car bucked as she steered it out onto the track. Stopping behind the starter line, she fixed her concentration on the trackman sitting on the fence. When the flag dropped, so did her foot, right to the floor, the other one releasing the clutch in the same instant. The car jumped at the sudden burst of energy, skidding slightly on the hard, shiny surface of the tarmac.

Bear stiffened but said nothing. He'd never been a copilot before, and he'd damn well never ridden with a woman who pulled him like a magnet. He took a deep breath and settled back, his body cocked just a hair so that he could keep his eyes on the road and the driver.

Rounding the first turn was relatively simple. He noted how she fed into the turn, braking rhythmically, then depressing the accelerator to bring herself smoothly out into the straightaway. Someone had tutored Kip Noble well in the elements of race driving.

On the straightaway he concentrated on the pull and power of the engine and wheel. They were as smooth as butter and worked together very sweetly.

Around and around the oval Kip drove, tires squealing, frame vibrating with unleashed power. Hugging the ground on every turn, and taking each one more forcefully than the last, Kip smiled, gaining confidence in herself and the machine.

Bear too was smiling. He would never have said he could be comfortable as a passenger in a race car, but he'd unbent a good deal riding with Kip Noble. Though she had a slender, delicate-looking frame, she was strong . . . and determined. She had to be to control the power that was under her hands.

His ears attuned to every nuance of a motor, he noticed the infinitesimal whine at once. "What the hell . . . ?" His voice was drowned out by the roar of the motor.

Kip felt the car drift. Surprise kept her from reacting for a second, then she straightened the car out. What had happened? Why? No time to analyze, not at the speed she was traveling. Cold perspiration beaded her body. She gritted her teeth, her gaze fixed on the course, looking for an escape, just in case . . .

Bear had almost expected the ping-ing sound that followed the whine. He braced himself.

"The car!" Kip yelled.

"I know," he shouted back. "Hold her. If she jumps I'll help."

All of Kip's efforts to slow the car were useless, and they hit the curve too fast. Shuddering, the car hydroplaned as centrifugal force pulled it toward the wall. Bear grabbed the wheel, fighting it with Kip. "We'll make it," he said between clenched teeth, though he knew she couldn't hear him.

Kip's body was drenched. They were going to die! Her peripheral vision showed the wall they were almost scraping. If it hadn't been for Bear's powerful hands wrestling the car into the next turn, they would have crashed into that wall.

Bear spotted an open area, marked by sundial-shaped flower beds in the middle of the flat grass verge. Beyond was rocky ground, but it was their best shot. "We're going through," he whispered.

"Yes," Kip said as though she'd heard him.

Four hands on the wheel steered a path through the dormant flower beds. The car furrowed the still brown lawn, then they were down a small gully into rougher ground.

"Brake!" Bear yelled just as Kip's foot went down. "Not too hard."

She batted at the brake as they plowed into a sea of ice-coated mud. The car spun around, its engine roaring like a furious beast.

"Accelerate!" Bear shouted.

Kip did.

They rocked and slid, then roared down an incline.

Vibrating in protest, the car skidded sideways, finally starting to slow. They screeched to a halt, their bodies thrown against the restraints of their seat belts.

Silence.

Bear shook himself, forcing his head to clear as the sound of sirens penetrated his dazed consciousness. Then he quickly turned off the engine and unstrapped himself and Kip.

After opening his door, he lifted her onto his lap and rolled out of the car, holding her tightly in his arms.

"I . . . can . . . walk," she said, panting, groggy.

"We're crawling," he told her, dragging her across the rough, cold ground, away from the car.

"Will it explode?"

"I hope not." He grunted, not releasing his grip as he felt the rocks tear at his jumpsuit.

As though on signal, a cacophony broke around them, yelling mixed with the screeching of brakes, sirens, and the thudding of running feet in a discordant medley. Suddenly people were all around them, spraying fire repellent over the car and the surrounding area.

Hands swept over Kip and Bear. Voices admonished them to stay still.

"Get her the hell out of here, Gunder," Bear managed to say as his friend bent over him.

"It's okay, Bear. We got it under control."

Bear glanced at the woman lying next to him. "You're a hell of a driver."

"So are you," she said.

He started to get up, but Gunder held him down, his chin jutting out determinedly. "Hey, Gunder, you know I'm not hurt. Let me up."

"I'm no doctor, and neither are you. You're going to the hospital. If you don't go quietly, I'll bust your jaw for you."

Bear heard Kip's low laugh and swiveled his head toward her. Her laughter was like the sound of a stream rushing over stones. It feathered up and down his spine. "You're going too, you know."

"Yes, but I won't have to be restrained." She frowned, looking past him to the car. "What happened?"

"Gunder will tell us in short order, if you let him take charge of the car."

Kip stared at him, inhaling a deep breath. Then she nodded her assent.

"I'll pick you up from the hospital," Gunder said, beginning to move toward the car. "Hey, hold on there. Don't touch nothin'," he yelled to the group of men gathered around it.

When one of Kip's mechanics started to protest, Kip called, "Let him go over the car, Marty. He's Gunder Bailey."

The men nodded and backed off.

"Ready to go, ma'am?" one of the paramedics asked Kip, bending over her.

She nodded and was placed on a gurney.

"You'll never lift me," Bear said, grinning at the three paramedics standing over him.

"No problem, sir," one said quietly.

In minutes Bear was in the ambulance with Kip.

Not all the questions the paramedics asked him kept Bear from watching Kip Noble. She was well named, he mused. Noble. There was a deep graciousness about her, a regalness, but an earthiness too. She intrigued the hell out of him . . . and he should stay away from her. When he was racing, he hadn't had time for any serious relationships. And he'd comforted enough widows of his friends not to want to put a woman in that position. His life had been simple, uncomplicated, with lovely women moving in and out of it. He liked it that way and didn't want to change it. Maybe Kip Noble would change it for him.

That thought jolted him, and he stiffened.

"What is it, sir? Did you get a sudden pain? Where?" Kip turned to him, concern etched on her fine features. "Do you think you did get hurt, Bear?"

That was the first time she'd called him by name. "No, I'm fine."

They were quiet for the rest of the journey.

The hospital emergency room was a maelstrom, and it was some time before a doctor verified that Kip and Bear had suffered only cuts and bruises.

Bear sat on the edge of his gurney, buttoning his shirt, when a swishing sound behind him told him someone had parted the curtain and entered his cubicle.

"I wondered if you wanted to share my taxi," Kip said.

He turned quickly, almost upsetting himself. He noticed that, though Kip stood straight, there was a slight rockiness to her. The effects of shock? "Thanks. I'd appreciate that." He tried to right himself and nearly slipped off the bed.

"Are you going to fall from there?" she asked.

Her gurgle of laughter turned his blood to water, his knees to soft butter. "Let me take you to dinner," he said.

She stared at him. "It's one o'clock in the afternoon."

"True, but we need to talk about the car . . . and if you're going to sell it to Kenmore Motors." He wanted to see more of her. If he had to use the car to do it, he would.

Kip smothered a sigh. Business. Her heart had leapt

into her throat at the invitation, and she told herself to smarten up. From all she'd heard, Bear gobbled up women like a killer whale gobbled up seals. She'd better stick to business. "My staff feels I would have better luck with some of the smaller companies—"

"Or even the foreign market. I know."

Bear fastened the last button on his shirt and stood. She turned to leave, but staggered. He put his hand out to steady her, smiling down at her.

"I always had the wobblies for a time after a crash," he said.

Her heart turned over at the smile. "I don't think I'd like to get used to that."

He shrugged. "You never do. I want to see you get to a comfortable place first, then we can talk if you like. Or you could rest and I could join you later."

"Thanks, but I'm feeling pretty solid. We can talk in the taxi."

"Capable, aren't you?" He wanted to cuddle her, cosset her, care for her.

She met his gaze and found herself unable to look away. "Yes, I'm capable. My uncle saw to that." Bear Kenmore was having a wild effect on her respiration. Her pulse was a drumbeat.

"Did he teach you how to stiff-arm the opposition too?" he asked.

"I learned that myself." She laughed. "Never been knocked down by a woman before?"

"Not that I can recall." Bear couldn't stop an answering smile. She charmed the hell out of him.

Kip's laughter grew louder as she stepped into the hall. A passing intern glanced at her and smiled.

Bear had an urge to knock him flat. He shook his head. Maybe he was feverish.

"Ready to go?" she asked. "I'm looking forward to a long, hot soak in the tub."

"I'd like a shower myself." He refused to indulge in the fantasy of Kip in a bubble bath.

"Let's go."

"Come to my town house, and I'll show you my cat Clancy and her baby Dyna."

"You called a female cat Clancy?"

"And Dyna's short for Dynamite." He took her arm and led her to the exit. "Come to my place and I'll show them to you."

"Said the spider to the fly," she murmured dryly. "Is this a new twist on the etchings scam?"

Bear stopped in the hospital corridor and spread his arms. "Look, ma, no hands. I promise I only want to show you my animals, and then we'll talk or part."

"How is it that you brought your pets to Michigan when your home is in New York?"

"I fly my own plane, and they like to travel."

Kip pursed her lips. "Why do I get the feeling you're either a consummate liar, or I've just been dragged through the looking glass?"

"Since I usually tell the truth, you must be Alice." He held the door for her, then whistled for a taxi that had just disgorged three people.

"Well, which is it?" he asked as he helped her in. "My place? Or do you wish to go directly to yours?"

She hesitated, then nodded. "I guess I have to see those remarkable cats."

Bear grinned and gave the driver his address.

Neither spoke during the ride as they looked out their windows. Yet each was overwhelmingly aware of the other.

Kip could not only hear his breathing, she could feel it.

Bear was sure her breath surrounded him, creating a new aura in the cab. He felt entrapped in a wonderful mystique.

The taxi stopped in front of a town house, set in the center of a neat row of town houses.

"It looks nice," Kip said as Bear paid the driver.

"I think so. Shall we go in?"

She nodded and walked beside him up five wide concrete steps to an ornate front door with beveled glass side windows.

Bear unlocked the front door, then opened the airlock door to an expansive foyer. Kip stepped into the foyer, then stopped dead as an enormous dog gamboled from the back of the house right at her.

"Good Lord," she breathed, bracing herself for an attack. She'd never seen a dog like that before. Was it man-eating? Panic had replaced reason.

"Sit, Dyna!" Bear commanded.

"Dyna," Kip said raggedly, as the panting canine slid across the hardwood floor, its rear plastered down and its fanlike tail sweeping the floor furiously. "You said Dyna was a kitten."

"No, you said that. I said Dyna was my cat's baby. She is. Clancy and I were walking through Central Park one day and Clancy found her, half-frozen by the lake. She'd been mauled by something, maybe other dogs, maybe a person. I don't know. I carried her back to my place, then Clancy washed her and comforted her all the way to the vet's. When we brought her home, Dyna just assumed Clancy was her mother and climbed into the cat's basket with her." Bear shrugged. "I've had to get several bigger baskets because I can't seem to break her of the habit."

"You're joking." Kip eyed the sleek black-and-white cat ambling from the back of the house, tail and chin high. She walked past the mammoth dog, rubbed against it, then casually jumped into Bear's arms.

"Mother and child," Bear said softly, petting the large feline.

"Have you considered Ripley's 'Believe It or Not'?" Kip leaned back a bit from the cat, who was eyeing her unblinkingly. Bear Kenmore was crazy, but he was also compassionate. If she'd felt any trepidation at accompanying him to his house, those feelings dissipated as she watched him with the cat and dog. He was kind! That rocked her.

"From what I've heard," he said, setting the cat on the floor, "it's not that unusual for a cat to adopt a dog."

Kip noticed his gentle handling of the cat, his firm but quiet way with the dog. She wasn't especially fond of animals, had never owned one, but she still felt a linkage to Bear Kenmore, one she couldn't explain.

"Are you afraid of animals?" he asked.

"No, but I can't say I know too much about them." She watched as the cat sauntered over to the dog, then stretched up on her hind legs to take hold of the dog's muzzle. "These two are fascinating. What kind of dog is Dyna?"

"A Great Pyrenees. I can put them in another room so they won't bother you."

"They don't bother me." She glanced at him. "May I use your bathroom?"

"Sure. This way." He led her up the stairs that hugged one wall of the two-story foyer, ordering the dog to the back of the house when she would have followed them.

On the second floor he gestured to a door. "That's the guest suite. Feel free to take a shower. I'll be back here, if you need me." He pointed toward another door at the far end of the hall.

She nodded and walked into the spacious suite. Done in cream and gold, it had a bedroom, sitting room, and full bathroom. Feeling grimy, she was tempted to shower. Even though she didn't have clean clothes to change into, she'd feel fresher after bathing.

Giving into temptation, she stripped off her things, draping them over the towel bars. Maybe the steam would take some of the wrinkles out of them, she thought, making a face at the clothes.

As she thoroughly scrubbed herself with shampoo and soap, Kip sighed with well-being. After toweling herself dry, she used the hair dryer to fluff up her natural wave and reapplied her makeup.

As she walked back into the sitting room, the phone rang. She assumed Bear would answer it, but after it had rung four times, she picked it up. "Hello?"

"Hello. This is Dolph Wakefield. Is Bear there?"

Was that Dolph Wakefield the movie star? she wondered. "Yes, but I assume he's in the shower. May I take a message?"

"Yes. Tell him dinner is on. We'll definitely be in New York tonight, Piers, Damiene, and I. And we can't wait to see him. He knows where to reach me if there's a problem. May I ask your name?"

"Yes. I'm Kip Noble."

"Nice meeting you, Kip Noble."

"Nice meeting you, Dolph Wakefield." She replaced the phone. Dolph Wakefield? Nah, couldn't be. Funny that two men should have such a distinctive name.

Leaving her suite, she walked to Bear's. She knocked twice on the door, but there was no answer. After a moment's hesitation, she opened the door. The room was empty, but she paused to look around it, impressed by the furnishings and decor in shades of blue, brown, and cream.

Just as she was turning to leave, the bathroom door opened and Bear was there. Naked as a jaybird, he strolled across the room to where a suit hung on a valet. He hadn't seen her.

Frozen in place, she watched him rub a towel over his wet hair as he studied the suit. "Sorry," she whispered.

He looked up and leisurely wrapped the towel around his waist. "Hi. Come in, Kip."

"I'm embarrassed. I shouldn't have just marched in here when you didn't answer the knock. I did knock."

He grinned. "I'm not embarrassed."

"I can see that," she said tartly, then blushed a deeper red.

"How far does that blush go?" he whispered.

"I took a call for you," she said, ignoring the question as a fresh rush of blood heated her face. She strode to the door. "I'll give you the message when you come downstairs," she told him, and started to leave.

A well-shaped hand on her shoulder stopped her. "Stay." Bear closed his eyes as he inhaled her essence, lowering his head so that his face touched her hair. "You have beautiful hair."

"I washed it with your shampoo." Why was breathing so difficult? she wondered. Her nose quivered with the fresh, soapy scent of him.

"You did say you had a message for me," he murmured.

"All right." She turned, then blinked. His mouth was centimeters from hers. His lips were moist, parted. It would be like jumping into an inferno to kiss him. "Back up."

Bear stared down at her, then nodded slowly. Though he liked having women in his life, his approach to them had always been casual. Moving away from Kip

Noble should have been a snap, yet it took all his resolve to do it.

As he stepped back, his towel slipped. Kip's eyes widened. Damn! he thought. He didn't want to scare her away.

"Wait over there by the window," he said. "I'll be right back."

Kip had hardly begun to regain her aplomb, to get her breathing back into proper rhythm, when he was back at her side, gray sweatpants hugging his lower body. "That was fast." It was hard even to smile at him without having the feeling that she was offering herself to him. The slightest movement he made quickened her heartbeat. Bear Kenmore happened to be one of those men who had a surfeit of sexual magnetism. And he was kind. That was highly dangerous.

He led her to a window seat and sat down with her. "Comfortable?"

Hell, no. "Yes. The call was from a man called Dolph Wakefield." Bear nodded. "He has the same name as the movie star."

"Same person, but don't let Dolph hear you call him a movie star. He considers himself an actor, though he hasn't done much of it lately."

"I saw him once on the stage, and several times in the movies. He's good."

"He's also a crack director and producer. Was anything wrong?"

"No. He was just confirming a dinner date with you and two people named Piers and Damiene."

"Great!" Bear exclaimed. "So, they'll be there. I was afraid he might be calling to say Damiene wasn't up to it." Bear's smile faded. "She's pregnant and we're worried about her. Her husband Piers convinced her to move to New York from their home in Nevada during the last trimester, because he felt she'd get better medical care there."

"Good friends of yours?" Kip was warmed by his concern for his friend, yet oddly felt left out.

"The best friends in the world," he said.

"Oh."

Bear leaned toward her. "Come to dinner with me in New York. I'll fly us back here tonight, or early tomorrow."

"What?" Had the world tipped off its axis?

"I want you to meet my friends, Kip. Come with me."

Two

Manhattan was beautiful. Kip should have been used to that, but it was always a surprise, even when she'd been away a short time. Though she commuted from Detroit regularly to visit the textile company she'd inherited from her uncle, she had gotten used to Detroit and Chicago.

Now that the test driving of the race car was over, she would be moving to Manhattan. The bulk of her business was there, and the commuting had become tiresome.

Upon her uncle's death she'd assumed the leadership of all of his businesses. For most of them, she assigned the everyday running to well-trusted vice presidents, while she put her energies into the car and the textile company, Morningstar Textiles.

Importing and fashioning fabrics had been an amusing sideline to her uncle, and he'd bought Morningstar almost whimsically, five years earlier when Kip was twenty-three. It had surprised both of them when Morningstar became a thriving business.

Kip had spent her last summer of business school working at the factory, learning the many facets of the business. After she received her master's, she worked with her uncle, yet spent the bulk of her time at Morningstar. When her uncle died, she was more or less running the textile company on her own.

Landing at La Guardia jolted her from her musings.

What had made her do such an unprecedented thing? she wondered, watching Bear as he skillfully handled the landing. Why had she consented to fly in a private plane with a veritable stranger to meet other strangers? Was she too young for a midlife crisis? Or was it simple, unadorned lunacy? As he'd driven her to her apartment so she could change and pack clothes for dinner, she'd told herself she was crazy to go with him. Yet as many times as she almost told him she'd changed her mind, something stopped her. It seemed so right to be with him. It was as though she'd known him for years, that they had a trusting and sound relationship. After mere hours? Ridiculous. Yet she couldn't shake the feeling that being with Bear was a very good idea. He was handsome, sexy, virile. But she'd known other men like that. Her ex-husband had those characteristics. Why was Bear different?

She heard the cat meow in its carrier behind her and smiled. She didn't know many men who would fly their pets around with them because animals liked to travel. And that was one of the reasons she found Bear Kenmore so intriguing. They'd called him Black Frost when he raced, but she'd seen a warm, caring side of him that had overridden all of her good reasons not to accompany him.

Landing at La Guardia could've been hairy. It was so busy. Kip was amazed at how smoothly Bear landed, had them deplane, and had gotten them into a limousine.

"Having second thoughts?" Bear asked once they were settled in his luxurious chauffeur-driven Rolls-Royce, speeding from Queens to Manhattan.

"Second, third, and fourth," Kip muttered, but a thrill of anticipation shivered up her spine. It would be interesting to see Bear interact with his friends. Would they like her?

He lifted her hand from her lap and kissed it. "No strings, no need to worry. Just a nice dinner with congenial people, then we're back on the plane and out of here." What would she say if he told her he was tempted to ask her to dinner the following night? Any place she chose. He rolled his shoulders as if his jacket constricted him. Things were going too fast, and he couldn't seem to steer a course. That didn't make him unhappy or ready to run, though, and that in itself was disturbing.

"Sounds simple," she said.

"It is." He loved her tremulous smile. She looked as fragile as a hothouse orchid, but he had seen her steel, her determination and courage. He hadn't driven against many men with more grit. Kip Noble was alluring, womanly, desirable, and tough as boots. What a paradox! "Tell me about the businesses you run." When her eyebrows lifted in question, he grinned. "You've been written up a few times since your uncle's death."

She smiled, hesitating, but it was hard to resist talking about the work she loved. "My uncle groomed me to take his place." She bit her lip. "Though I was sure I would be an old woman before I did. Most of the companies are small, but they pay their way. We've a computer-games company, a roller-skating factory, and a small chain of music stores. They all show a profit. Designing cars had been a hobby with Uncle Phineas, and it grew into a profitable business. There haven't been many cars, but the concepts have been good and have paid off. I think the latest will too." She frowned.

"Problems?"

"Oh, a man by the name of Richard Granger has been pressuring me since my uncle died." She glanced at Bear, then looked away. "He wants to buy Morningstar Fabrics . . . and he mentioned the car as well. He's come to my office and called several times, even though I've told him I'm not interested."

Bear frowned. "Call security and have him thrown out of your office if he comes around again."

Kip laughed, feeling lighthearted as she pictured the blustering Mr. Granger being tossed out on his ear. "Well, he hasn't called lately. So maybe he's accepted the inevitable."

"What sort of fabrics do you sell?" He smiled at how her face lit up, how eagerly she turned to him.

"Some we import from the Orient, India, and the Middle East. But some are fashioned right here. We have silks of all kinds, worsteds, linens, and some man-made fabrics that are getting better and better. We're wholesalers who sell to the retail companies, or to decorating firms, furniture manufacturers, clothiers, that sort of thing."

"Sounds big."

"We're growing." She felt shy all at once. She'd been chattering. "Tell me about Kenmore Motors."

"We're growing too, and diversifying. It's a form of protection. Cars were always the core of the company, but we're into real estate and fiber optics now, and a few other smaller interests." He squeezed her hand. "Here we are."

When the Rolls pulled up in front of a charming brownstone on Manhattan's upper east side, Kip turned to look at him. "Another place?"

Bear shrugged. "Actually this is my home base. My business runs out of Manhattan."

"But isn't Kenmore Motors mainly in Detroit?"

He nodded. "But as I said, the business has expanded to include other industrial disciplines, making it more feasible to work out of New York."

Kip was going to say more, but the chauffeur was holding the door, so she followed Bear out of the car. "Thank you for the ride through Manhattan," she told the driver. "I enjoyed it."

"Thank you, miss." The driver smiled at her.

Bear studied her. She had the magic. The last time he'd seen Phelps smile that way was when he beat a Porsche away from a light. "We'll be going out in an hour," he told Phelps.

"I figured that, Bear. Piers called twice. I told him that with Lady Damiene in her last trimester, he's jumpier than a cat on a hot tin roof."

"Trust you to tell him that," Bear said dryly.

"No sense in not tellin' him," Phelps said as he took their overnight bags out of the trunk. He jerked his thumb at the two animals in their carriers in the back. "I'll take them with me while I park, then bring them in myself."

Kip chuckled as Phelps opened the driver's door. "I like him."

Bear gave her a sour look. "Don't tell him, please. I have enough problems with him."

"I heard that," Phelps said as he slipped back under the wheel. "Gunder said the lady outdrove you today." Phelps gunned the engine, drowning out Bear's monosyllabic response.

"Don't grin that way," Bear said to Kip, though he was smiling too. He couldn't quite mask the delight he felt listening to her laugh.

"He seems to know you well," she said as she preceded him up the steps to the door. His reluctant smile touched her heart like a plucked string, the reverberation going all through her. Was it possible to be virile man and small boy at the same time? Bear Kenmore was appealing . . . and sexy . . . and powerful. She enjoyed being with him.

"He was another mechanic who worked for me." Bear frowned for a moment.

"And he's your friend."

He unlocked the door and ushered her in. "He saved my life. He and Gunder ripped open a car, literally, with their bare hands. It was on fire, and I was trapped inside. Both of them suffered more severe burns than I did."

Kip watched the play of emotions on his face, as though a horror film was unwinding in the front of his brain. What made her curl her hand into his, she didn't know.

Bear's hand tightened around hers. Did she know? he wondered. Had she seen the nightmares that were always there, just under the surface? The flames curling around the three of them as Phelps and Gunder struggled to get him out of the car. He'd screamed at them to leave him, but they'd stayed, tearing and ripping until he was free and away from the inferno. The heat from the explosion had burned the clothes from their backs.

"This is quite grand," Kip said, drawing him from his tortuous memories. "Have you lived here long?"

He glanced around the long, narrow entryway, its parquet floor gleaming. To the left they could just see into his library, with its thick Oriental rug and large mahogany desk. "My father purchased it about twenty years ago from a family who'd owned it since around 1850. I bought it from him when I quit racing."

She stroked the marble top of a side table. "Nice furniture too," she said, and sent him a sidelong glance.

He smiled. "I do not steal for a living—"

"At least not overtly."

"I earned the money to buy this house—"

"Race drivers make good money," she agreed politely, enjoying the exchange. Challenging Bear Kenmore was fun.

"Why do I feel I have to explain to you?" he muttered. Why did she mean so much to him? He'd just met her. "Next I'll be showing off for you like a schoolboy."

"Why are you mumbling?" She couldn't contain her amusement.

"Come on, I'll show you your room." He was definitely out of his mind, he thought. He was two shades away from begging for her approval of his home, of him. There must be a clinic somewhere that dealt with twenty-four-hour disintegration of the mind.

"We're going back tonight, though," she said. "Right?" Survival meant getting the messages straight, being up-front . . . standing on her own.

"Right." Why did the thought of taking her back to Detroit bother him?

Bear showed her into a guest bedroom on the third floor. "I'll make some calls. If you want to freshen up, there's everything you need."

"Thank you." What had furrowed his brow and tightened his mouth? she wondered. Regret that he had brought her?

Bear retraced his steps back downstairs to his library. He dialed a familiar number and, when the phone was answered, said, "Hello, Piers."

"Bear, how are you? Are you in town?"

"Yes, I'll be there for dinner . . . and I'll be bringing someone, if that's all right with you."

"Fine," Piers said.

When Bear hung up, he called Gunder. "Any more on the car?"

"Not yet. It was definitely the carburetor and brakes that went. I'm still trying to figure out why. Or how. You're worried."

"I am."

"I'll hurry it along."

Piers Larraby replaced the bedroom phone as his wife came out of the bathroom. His smile softened as he looked at her bulbous body. "You're beautiful, wife."

"Anyone who could think a woman who looked like Dumbo the elephant was beautiful has a problem."

He opened his arms to her, and she walked into them, serene and confident in his love. After he'd kissed her thoroughly, she asked, "Was that Bear on the phone?"

"Yes, he's joining us for dinner, and he's bringing someone."

"And that bothers you?"

"Actually it doesn't, but he sounded strange. There was a surprise, a kind of shock in his voice. Maybe a little anger."

Damiene giggled. "My big Bear upset by anything? Never."

Piers kissed her hard. "Why is that so unbelievable? You upset me all the time."

"And you are making mountains out of molehills with this pregnancy."

"I'm a careful man." He kissed her again, his hands sweeping over her.

"Everything is fine," she soothed.

He held her tighter. "I'll make sure of that."

•   •   •

Kip noticed how withdrawn Bear became as they drove through Manhattan later that evening. "Where are we going?"

Silence.

"He's nervous," Phelps informed her gleefully. "You've made quite an impact on him. Maybe it's your revolutionary auto." He laughed.

"You cackle like an old hen," Bear told his friend before pressing the button that raised the glass, separating the driver and the passengers.

"Are you nervous?" Kip asked.

"No . . . yes. I don't know. I have to think about it."

Temper erupted in her. "I could have stayed home. That might have kept you in a better frame of mind."

Startled, Bear turned to look at her. For a long moment they stared at each other. The air seemed to vibrate with suppressed desire. As if unable to stop herself, Kip leaned toward him. His gaze flicked to her lips, then he gathered her into his arms, his mouth coming down on hers in a warm, searching kiss.

Surprise rendered her limp for a moment; then she struggled to be free. An instant later, though, she didn't want to be free. Knowing that shocked her more than the kiss. Her arms had a life of their own as they twined around his strong neck, her mouth opening beneath his naturally. Pleasure coursed through her, and she pressed closer to him.

Bear recognized all the signs of arousal. They'd been part of his life since adolescence. The new and alien sensation was the urge to cherish and protect Kip. Why should he feel that way toward a very independent woman? Bear couldn't answer that. He only knew that he would have stood in front of a bus for Kip, and that he would have stopped it.

"Ahem, I hate to interrupt, but we're here," said a gleeful Phelps.

Bear tore his lips from Kip's and wheeled on his friend. "Go . . . to the . . . George Washington . . . Bridge and . . ." Out of breath and struggling with his cataclysmic emotions, he could only glare at Phelps.

"It's still pretty wintry, Bear. I ain't jumpin'." Phelps chuckled. "I like you like this. You're in about eighteen pieces, right? Good for you. Thanks for coming along, Miss Noble. You've done a real job on him." Phelps laughed again.

Bear growled deep in his throat, sounding like the animal whose name he carried.

"We'd better go," Kip said hurriedly, embarrassed at her actions and shocked by her feelings.

"Yes," Bear said, more shaken than he cared to admit.

"I'll pick you up at eleven," Phelps instructed them.

"I'm calling a cab," Bear said murderously.

"Suit yourself. This is more comfortable."

"No, it isn't."

Phelps was still chuckling as he got back into the car and drove away.

"This is a beautiful street," Kip said, looking around. "I didn't know they had homes like this in this city, even down here in Greenwich Village."

"Some of these homes date back to revolutionary days," Bear said absently, still struggling to regain his equilibrium.

"Oh."

He smiled, glad to see she was as nonplussed as he.

He walked her to the door, then leaned down to kiss her swiftly. "You're very beautiful, Kirsten Patricia Noble."

She lifted one hand to touch his face. "You're all right, too, Bear Kenmore. But," she added, "I am going back to Detroit tonight."

"I know that."

But he wasn't going to let her go, he vowed. Confused and aroused, he stared at her, as if he'd find the answer to his turbulent emotions in her eyes.

Neither heard the door swing open or noticed the interested gaze fixed on them.

"Whenever you're ready, I am," Dolph Wakefield said. "It's damned cold with the door open."

When Kip would have moved away from him, Bear tightened his hold on her. "Go to hell, Dolph," he said easily.

"I'll get there eventually," Dolph said, his gaze on Kip. "Won't you come in, Miss Noble? I'm afraid my friend's manners are deplorable."

"I hate it when you do your Oxford imitation," Bear said.

"Tough." Dolph grinned, then turned to Kip and introduced himself.

"I read somewhere that you went to school in Europe," Kip said shyly. Dolph Wakefield was even more breathtakingly handsome in person than on the screen. He was quite tall, with streaked blond hair and dark green eyes. "Or is that hype?"

"All true," Bear said with relish, knowing his friend hated to discuss himself. "Maybe he'll tell you about the time he read a paper for one of the learned professors at Heidelberg. Distinguished career and all that rot."

"Release her, will you, Bear?" Dolph said as he closed the door behind them. "I just want to take her coat."

"I'll take care of it," Bear said, removing Kip's wrap.

"Fine." Dolph waited until Bear had the coat in the air, then he whisked Kip away from him and down a short hall. "You handle the coats. I'll take care of Kip."

"Dolph! Let her go."

"No way." Dolph looked down at Kip. "He's a little irked."

"It's good for him," she said, chuckling.

Muttered curses followed them into the spacious living room.

"He's going to kill me," Dolph said genially to the tall, dark-haired man leaning on the mantel and the woman, obviously pregnant and with lovely silver-blond hair and turquoise eyes, seated on a love seat.

Piers straightened, his gaze moving from Kip to Dolph. "Oh?"

Dolph grinned. "Bear is acting like his namesake."

Bear strode into the room at that moment. Though he was smiling, he held himself stiffly. Kip could feel the tension rolling off him. "I owe you," he said softly to Dolph.

"I can sympathize," Piers said. "Even empathize."

Bear didn't answer, but walked across the room to the woman sitting on the love seat. "Hello, beautiful lady. How are you feeling?"

"Fine. Are they teasing you?"

"They think they are." He kissed her gently, then walked back to Kip. Effectively freeing her from Dolph, he led her to the love seat. "Kip, this is Damiene Larraby, Piers Larraby, and Dolph Wakefield."

"Stop acting like a tornado," Kip said. "I'm getting dizzy." She hadn't meant to sound censorious, and when the other men laughed, she wished she'd bitten her tongue.

"Oh? Do you think you can control him?" Dolph asked, moving to the bar in one corner of the spacious living room.

"Dolph!" Damiene glanced at the man, who nodded, smiling ruefully.

"All right, Damy, I'll be good," Dolph promised.

"Me too." Piers bent down to kiss his wife.

"Don't stop on my account," Kip said, reading the scenario that had begun between the friends. "Anything that pulls Bear down a peg has my vote."

"Traitor," Bear whispered in her ear.

She smiled.

"Your name sounds familiar, Kip," Piers said. "Are you related to Phineas Noble?"

"He was my uncle." She glanced at Bear. "That's how we met. Bear was at the test driving of my uncle's last car this morning."

Piers and Dolph exchanged glances, then Dolph asked, "Did you let him drive?"

"Kip drove," Bear answered. "I was the passenger."

The ice Dolph had been holding with tongs clattered back into the bucket. "You? A passenger? Come on, don't try to fool us. We know you."

"She drove me. Ask Gunder."

"I will," Piers said slowly, his gaze lingering on Kip.

Much to Kip's relief, Damiene steered the conversation in another direction.

"Tell us about the new film you'll be doing in China, Dolph."

"All right, Damy." He grinned at her, knowing what she was doing. "We don't start shooting for another three months, so I'll be here for the baby's birth."

"You did get them to push it back, then?" Bear asked.

"Yes. I figured I'd be a nervous wreck on the other side of the world with Damy delivering."

The three men nodded, and Damiene winked at Kip. "Aren't they a hoot, Kip? They think if they're around, it should go much easier for me."

"Oh, I'm sure it will," Kip said sardonically.

The three men nodded vigorously.

"They believe it," she said faintly.

Bear frowned. "Of course we believe it. We're all going to be there for her."

"Will you make room for the obstetrician?"

Damiene laughed. "They aren't kidding, you know, and they have no sense of humor on the subject."

The three men opened their mouths to comment, when a man dressed in stark black announced dinner.

Kip tried not to stare.

"That's Cosmo, the general factotum," Damiene explained to Kip, who was trying not to stare. "He's a former wrestler who cooks for Dolph, but who also guards me when I come to town." She smiled as Piers helped her to her feet. "Sometime I'll tell you about what happened to Piers and me. It's long over, but he still gets jumpy. Unfortunately, he has the blessing of my parents in all he does, so I'm outvoted."

"And I'll bet the three musketeers band together to care for you," Kip said as she walked with Damiene to the dining room.

"They're ridiculous, but I love them. You'll grow to love the three of them too."

Kip jerked her head around to stare at Damiene. "But Bear and I—I mean . . ."

"Maybe I'm rushing my fences a bit," Damiene said, "but I'm not blind. Bear is one of the most gentle and strong men I've ever known. I love him dearly."

"He's . . . very interesting," Kip said lamely.

"Yes," Damiene said. "You know, I fell in love with Piers almost the moment we met. I didn't admit it, of course, and it was very uncomfortable at first. But I got used to it." She smiled as her husband pulled out her chair in the ornate, high-ceilinged dining room.

Kip stared at Damiene as Bear seated her. Rushing fences? Damiene Larraby was leaping tall buildings.

"What is it?" Bear asked, leaning over her. "You're pale. Do you feel all right?"

"Probably."

"What?"

"What? Oh, nothing." Kip looked around the room, then glanced down the table to Dolph. "This is a beautiful house. I never realized places like this were tucked away in New York. I've seen such houses in Philadelphia, but not here."

Dolph nodded. "This house has been in my family, in one way or another, since the Revolutionary War. My ancestors were Tories. Some of them returned to England when Washington's army won. After several years in England a few returned and claimed the property as their own. Of course, things have changed greatly since then." He smiled at Kip. "But there are quite a number of these places in the area. Since they're mostly single-family dwellings, they're virtually unknown."

Cosmo began serving the soup, and Bear saw Kip's eyes widen when she looked at a large abstract painting on the wall. "Marc Chagall," he whispered. "Beautiful, isn't it?"

"Very," she murmured.

"I know I shouldn't keep it here," Dolph said, "but my father bought it, and it has sentimental value." He shrugged, staring at the painting. "I've about made up my mind to donate it to the Metropolitan Museum of Art."

Damiene nodded. "Good idea. I've lost sleep thinking about that painting being stolen, or the house burning." She shuddered. "Get it to the museum."

They all turned their attention to the creamy shrimp bisque, and Bear smiled as Kip began to unwind. Damiene's naturalness relaxed her. By the time the entree of médaillons de veau was served, she was conversing freely with his friends.

"You're in bad shape, friend," Dolph said softly to him, midway through the meal.

Piers overheard the comment and chuckled. "I can't tell you how good that makes me feel, Bear."

Bear was about to tell Piers what he could do with his good feeling when Dolph intervened. "Maybe now isn't the time," he said in a low voice, "but Gunder called just before you arrived." His gaze slid from Bear to Piers. "You tell him."

"What?" Bear asked tautly.

"If I understand Gunder fully," Piers said, "the brakes had been tampered with, and the carburetor ingeniously fouled." He glanced at Kip. "Someone want her out of the way? Or is it just the car?"

"Either way it could be dangerous," Dolph said.

Turning to him, Kip heard his remark. "What could be?" she asked.

The three men merely gazed at her for a moment, and Bear could see awareness dawn. Her features tightened suddenly, as though a string had been pulled inside her.

Slowly she faced him. "Did your mechanic discover that someone had tampered with the car?"

"Yes." Bear clenched his fists when she paled.

"Why didn't you tell me?" A trembling assaulted her body. Why would anyone tamper with her car? It was horrible.

"I just found out myself," Bear said, wishing he knew how to quell the turmoil he could see building in her.

"Tell me everything." She had to struggle to keep her voice steady. Someone had sabotaged the car! She and Bear could have been killed.

"Dolph would have to do that. He took the call."

"The brakes were fixed so that depressing them lightly didn't do any harm, but once you tramped down on them, they wouldn't hold."

Trepidation trickled through her. She didn't even try to answer Dolph. Who had done this? Why?

Damiene took her hand. "It's a little frightening when you think someone's after you." She smiled around the table. "But these three are the ones you want on your side. They were in my corner."

"Still are," Bear said softly.

Damiene laughed. "That's only because you'll be god-fathering our child."

"I'm a godfather too," Dolph said.

"Of course."

Kip tried to smile with them. She knew they were trying to lighten her mood, but she couldn't get her mind off the car. Why would anyone hate it so much? Or her?

Though she joined in the conversation after dinner, she couldn't get the car out of her mind.

On the way home Bear closed the window between Phelps and them and turned to her. "Tell me."

She looked at him. "Don't pretend to know me. You don't."

"I'm trying."

She shook her head, her anger dissipating. "I'm sorry. I don't mean to be snappish. It's just too confusing. Why would anyone sabotage my car? I don't have that many enemies. I pay my bills, usually on time."

He put his arm around her, ignoring her resistance as he pulled her close. "Don't blow this out of proportion, Kip. For one thing, we were pretty shaken up in that crash, even if we didn't get hurt. That can color things. Two, we don't have a complete accident report. So let's wait until we do."

Though he held her lightly, his blood was pounding through his veins. It was as though Kip herself was in his bloodstream. He'd watched her throughout dinner, and his desire for her had grown. She had been a warm and gracious guest, a consummate lady. But that was surface. There was so much more to Kirsten Patricia Noble. He wanted to know it all.

Kip had never felt so comfortable, yet how could a sexy, sensual man like Bear Kenmore make her feel relaxed?

"Are you married?" she asked abruptly, then closed her eyes in embarrassment. Where had that come from? Why hadn't she asked him before she'd come to New York with him? She could feel his chest move under her cheek as he laughed.

"Out of the blue you ask that question? No, I'm not married. Been close a time or two, but haven't done it. Actually, I never thought it would be fair to a woman or to me. Up until a few years ago, my life was traveling the racing circuit around the world." He paused. "And I've seen too many friends die, leaving their wives and children bereft. That's a nightmare."

She could feel his iron control. It was as though he'd frosted over for a second. "And it must have hurt to lose those friends."

"Yes," he murmured into her hair. And it had added a coldness to his soul as he'd promised himself never to put a woman in such a position. How quickly everything had turned around when he met Kip Noble. It jolted him to realize he could have given up racing for her, if he'd been still driving. She could melt him!

"Are you married?" he asked.

"We're certainly a little late with the questions, aren't we?" She turned and smiled up at him. "I married a few years ago. It didn't work out. We had what could be called a 'weekend marriage.' I was in Detroit, and he was here in Manhattan. Most weekends he'd fly to Michigan to see me. I think we both realized that what we had was single faceted with no deep roots. It didn't break up, it just petered out. He's an engineer and businessman, and he spends a great deal of time out of the country."

Jealousy wasn't green, Bear realized. It was crackling black ice, with a heart of ebony fire. "I see."

"You sound hoarse. Are you getting a cold?"

"Something like that." Aware that she was looking at him with puzzlement, he kissed her cheek. "Don't mind me. I'm just being stupid."

Kip knew there was no stupidity behind that face, but she didn't press him. Still, by the time they were airborne more than an hour later, Bear still wasn't talking. The black sky with its scudding gray clouds seemed a perfect setting for his mood.

"I hope you can fly properly when you're in a bad mood," she said with irritation as Manhattan faded behind them.

"I'm not in a bad mood. I'm just learning how to deal with jealousy. I don't like it, and it's not easy."

"Oh." Shock held her immobile. He hadn't even hedged with her.

"How long were you married?" he asked.

"About a year. We went our separate ways with mutual relief. I talk to him from time to time, but rarely see him."

"Good. Now what do we do about us?"

"What 'us'? Bear, we only met a few hours ago."

"I want to see more of you. What do you want?"

"I don't know. I'm all at sea. What do we know about each other?"

"Enough for the moment. But I want to know all of you."

"If someone is after the car, I don't think I'm a good person to know." She couldn't stem a shiver as she remembered the "accident."

"We're talking about our feelings here, Kip, not whatever situation we might find ourselves in. Let's be straight with each other."

"I would like to get to know you." The words were a waterfall of urgency. "But . . . I still don't know if it's a good idea."

"Don't sound so testy, Kip. I haven't asked for your car."

"You wouldn't get it."

"There you go again, biting off my head."

"Hah! I'm not as bad as you."

"I haven't had a conversation like this since adolescence."

"Me either."

Bear reached out a hand. Kip put hers into it.

"We'll go to movies," he said softly.

"And the opera."

"And have a soda."

"Right." She turned to look at him. "And it could get easier since I'll be moving to Manhattan soon."

Relief and joy flooded through him. "That would suit me, though I could transfer the bulk of my work to Detroit, if the need arises." He grinned at her. "We are going to have fun." He saw her smile slip for a moment, her eyes darken. "What is it?"

"My uncle used to say that when he purchased a company. 'We're going to have fun, Kip.' "

Bear touched her hair. "A very special man." When she nodded, he caressed her cheek.

"Most people would agree with you," she said. "Uncle Phineas was a man of impulse. And he had the Midas touch, I guess. Many of his ventures turned to wealth." She rested her head against the back of the seat. "Not that he paid much attention to that. He enjoyed the gamble, but he let others do the day-to-day work. Except for the cars, of course. He was on the job with them most of the time."

"He sounds like quite a man."

"He was. Morningstar Fabrics was one of the companies he'd bought on a whim. He was always doing things like that. He would get money from an invention, and he'd go out and squander some, invest some, and save a little. Sometimes his investments were crazy, but they generally paid off. Morningstar Fabrics was one of his weirder choices. But I'm glad he purchased it. I love the work."

"You were fond of him."

"Very. Phineas Noble was a gentle, kind genius. He was all the family I had, and I miss him very much. It seems like yesterday, not a year, since his death." She inhaled shakily. "I met my husband through Uncle Phineas. They were both trying to buy Morningstar as an investment property. Uncle Phineas made the right offer, I guess. Maybe he was sorry for Marsh because he lost out, so Uncle Phineas brought him home for dinner one night."

"His name's Marsh?"

"Yes. Marshall Finewood. His family has an importing business, specializing in Persian rugs. He has degrees in business and engineering. After our divorce I heard he went off to build roads or some such thing in South America."

"Did you have children?"

"No. We weren't married that long."

He didn't bother to hide his smile. He was delighted to know she hadn't had children with her husband. And he needed time to sort that out, as well as the many other emotions the compelling Miss Noble aroused in him.

"I'd like to learn to fly," she said after he'd landed in Detroit in a rush of power.

"I'll teach you."

She smiled at him. "I'll hold you to that."

"Do."

Since there was little traffic, the drive to her apartment was quiet. Bear walked her to her door, carrying
her small overnight bag. "Could we have dinner tomorrow night?" he asked. "Or the next?"

"Not tomorrow, but the next day would be fine." She
put out her hand.

He looked down at it, then shook it firmly. "Good
night. Thank you for a lovely evening."

"Isn't that my line?" She didn't even try to pull her
hand free.

"Maybe." He suddenly swept her into his arms and
kissed her, his mouth urgent on hers, fire building in
him. " 'Night."

"Good night." Reeling with a wild electricity, Kip was
barely able to unlock her door and step inside.

Bear ran back down the steps and got into his car,
not looking back. He might have returned to her if he
had. How he got to his place safely, he didn't know.

As soon as he was home, he called Gunder. "Hi. I
know it's late, but run that report by me."

"You're . . . out of . . . your mind." Gunder yawned,
rattled some papers, then began reading.

When he was through, Bear ground his teeth. "And
you don't think it could have just been stress, or any
other malfunction that caused the brakes to go and the
carburetor to act up?"

"Hell, no."

"I didn't say anything to Phelps."

"I called him, Bear. He has a right to know you were
in the accident, even if you weren't driving."

Bear slept fitfully that night, and was edgy and restless the next two days, eager to see Kip again.

By the time he reached her place, he was as nervous

as a boy on his first date. When she answered the door, he just stared at her.

The navy silk suit was plain, the jacket short, the skirt pencil-slim, complementing the low-heeled, navy-and-white spectator pumps. She should have looked businesslike, professional. To Bear she looked sensuous, sexy, and gorgeous.

"Come in. I just want to get my purse." As Kip was picking up the envelope purse that matched her shoes, the phone rang. "Hello? Oh, Marsh, how are you? I didn't know you were back. Oh, I'm fine. You read about it in the paper? I see. No, the car wasn't too powerful for me. Even Bear Kenmore said I drove well. Yes, it was a good thing he was there. Everything is great. Thank you for thinking of me. What? A rug show with the Marlowe Museum? Novel idea. When? I'll try to come. I'll be living in New York by then. Yes, permanently. In about two weeks. All right, good-bye." When Kip turned away from the phone and looked at Bear, she could barely control a shiver. His eyes were blue Arctic ice. "Shall we go?"

"Yes," Bear said abruptly. That had been her husband. Damn! Why couldn't he have stayed out of the country? "You'll be seeing your husband now that he's back in the States?" He could have bitten his tongue in two for asking that question.

"My ex-husband," she corrected him, wondering at his harsh tone. "But Marsh and I parted amicably. We might see each other." She didn't tell Bear that she avoided Marsh's friends, having nothing in common with them. Instead she strode past him out the door, her chin in the air.

The evening went downhill from there. It was as though a plastic barrier had risen between them. Inanities slipped from their mouths; their lips stretched in small smiles and snapped back again.

Kip didn't know what she ate.

Bear had three martinis, even though alcohol gave him a headache.

They left the restaurant early and barely talked on the ride home.

"I have to go to Europe on business," Bear said abruptly as he walked her to her door. "I'll be gone a couple of weeks." He wanted to ask her if he could call while he was away, yet said nothing.

"I see. Don't work too hard."

"I won't." Rigidly he turned and left her.

Kip was as frozen as he as she closed her door, too iced over even to cry.

Three

Kip didn't hear from Bear for two weeks, yet she dreamed about him each night. She saw his face on the street, at work, on other men. Anger didn't blot him out.

The night before she was to leave for New York, her phone rang. "It's Bear. I understand you're driving yourself to New York. Would it be all right if I drove you? I can get the right vehicle."

Nonplussed, Kip groped for all the reasons why she should say no. "Ah, all right . . ."

"See you tomorrow around nine."

She stared at the phone until the warning signal reminded her to hang up.

The next day was chaos. Kip had never figured moving to New York would be so involved, so messy, so frustrating.

After the movers left, she stood in her living room looking at the boxes she was supposed to get into her car. She shook her head.

When the doorbell rang, she rolled her eyes. It couldn't be the movers again, and it was too early for Bear.

She flung open the door and stared. "I didn't expect you until a little later."

"It's a beautiful day to make an early start."

"That's right, it is."

They stared at each other. Bear sucked in a deep breath. He'd given her space and time, and she'd marched through his mind day and night. How many times had he picked up the phone in London, Paris, and Hamburg, only to replace the receiver without calling her? He'd promised himself he wouldn't pressure her, and he hadn't.

"It was Gunder who told me you were moving today."

"How did Gunder know?" His features seemed to tighten, as though he were readying himself for a fight. "How?" she whispered.

"Since the accident with the car, I've told him to keep an eye on you," Bear said roughly.

She shook her head, stunned. "I didn't know."

"I know that. I was afraid you'd be intimidated. He called me with a report every night while I was in Europe." He didn't tell her he'd paced the floor each evening until he got the call.

"Oh." Uncertain what to say, she studied him from head to foot. The jeans and plaid shirt he wore gave him a stevedore toughness that was far different from the smooth, Gucci-shod man who ran Kenmore Motors and had taken her out to dinner.

"I brought an RV," he said, "so that we can hook your car to the back and load your gear in the storage area." His features tightened again. "If that's all right with you."

Feeling as if she'd stepped into a whirlwind, Kip walked to the window and looked down. A small RV was parked in front of the apartment building. "It's all right with me."

"Are these ready to go down?"

She turned, noting his arms piled with boxes. "Yes . . . but . . . but, the car . . ."

Bear watched her for a moment. They were like dogs circling each other. He should be kissing her, not bandying words with her. "Put the keys in my pocket and tell me where it's parked."

Kip hesitated, then went to get her keys. Returning to the living room, she said, "You didn't have to do this."

"I know." He leaned over the top of the boxes and kissed her lips lightly. "I looked forward to it."

Delight flooded her. He wanted to be with her . . . and she wanted to be with him. Insanity! She tried to muster all the anger and frustration she'd been aiming at him since their disastrous dinner, but she couldn't. After he'd gone, she stared at the door for long moments. Bear Kenmore was back. It was a jubilant refrain in her mind.

Hurriedly, she checked the apartment once more, then returned to the living room. He was there, holding the rest of the boxes. "I'm ready," she said.

He nodded. "Let's roll."

She followed Bear out the door and locked it behind her. She wasn't sorry to be leaving the apartment. Her short marriage had been spent there, and it was good to put it, and all its ramifications, behind her.

Bear loaded the boxes, then they climbed into the large bucket seats.

"What's that holding the car in the back?" she asked.

"It's a hitch we've used in towing racing cars. Very efficient."

"Oh."

Why were they so stilted with each other? he wondered. Why couldn't he speak as plainly to her as he did to Gunder or Phelps? Why couldn't she speak as naturally to him as she had to her doorman?

"Kip . . . I've missed you like hell," he said tautly, snapping on his safety belt.

She burst out laughing. "Is that why you're so grim?"

"No. Yes. You throw me off stride, lady."

"Well, you do the same to me." It was a relief to admit that to him . . . and to herself.

He shot a quick smile her way. "Let's enjoy this trip. Maybe we can get to know each other. I don't want to stay so far away from you anymore."

She turned in the seat to face him. "I wish I'd known that."

"I had the feeling I was crowding you. I thought you'd welcome some space."

"I thought so too." She'd missed him horribly.

He grinned, relaxing. "Want to drive?"

"No," she said, not quite able to stem an answering smile. "I guess you might do all right."

"All right? You know how to hurt a guy."

"Just a prick in his ego, to let out the air."

"Spicy-tongued brat."

She could hear the laughter in his voice. It was as though they'd started over, made a new beginning, met each other on a new plateau. "I think I could like you."

He glanced at her. "It's a start."

"Yes."

Driving the expressways could have been hairy with the car attached to the back, but Bear drove easily, comfortably, making it obvious he enjoyed driving.

"Tell me about racing," she said.

Bear's heart leapt up into his throat, then down again. She didn't mean the frosty black shadows, so he wouldn't mention those. "It was a game with me."

The huskiness in his voice told her there was more to it than that. "A rough game."

"Yes." A car careening across the track, engulfed in flames. There was no way out, no chance to save himself. Fire so hot it melted his suit to his body. Choking on the smoke, poisonous air ballooning in his brain, blinding him. Pain throbbing against his skull—

"You liked it until it began to take away something from you."

The remark she'd thrown into the air was like a silken thread a spider tosses. Out, then back again. Bear felt the silk encircle him. "Yes. It took my friends . . . and some of me."

Kip saw his hands tighten on the wheel. "I'm digging too deeply."

"Yes," he said unevenly, reaching out with one hand to touch her. "But I don't resent it, Kip. I just haven't talked that much about it." He shot her a quick glance. "It's something I've wanted to hide. You seem to know me very well. What do you think that means?"

"I make good guesses?"

He shook his head. "More than that, I think."

"I think so too. I think we all want to bury the pain. Sometimes we succeed. When I discovered my marriage wasn't all that I'd dreamed it could be, I became angry and withdrawn. I blamed Marsh and I blamed myself, but I couldn't verbalize my feelings to anyone." She inhaled a shuddering breath. "Until now."

He squeezed her hand. "Thanks. Maybe I'll be able to tell you all about racing one day."

Kip looked out the window, not able to say anymore. She hadn't seen him in a couple of weeks, then he waltzed back into her life and her heart went pitty-pat. And she unburdened her soul as she'd never done to another person. Insane!

"What's making you frown?" he asked.

"*You.*"

"Oh. Well, maybe we could talk about that over dinner. I know a nice place outside Cleveland."

"Cleveland? We should be long past there by evening."

"I thought we'd take our time."

She laughed. "We could speed."

"Spoilsport."

"Slowpoke." She looked about her. "This is my first time in a vehicle like this. I like the spacious feeling."

"Like to drive it?"

She nodded. "I'll spell you."

"Thank you, ma'am. Since I know how well you handle an automobile, I'll let you."

Inordinate pleasure rippled through her at his praise. "Thank you, I'd like that." She unstrapped herself. "Can I look in back?"

"Sure, but be careful. I don't like you moving around loose when I'm driving."

"All right, Daddy, I'll be careful."

"Cute, very cute." He chuckled as he glanced into the large rearview mirror. He could see her walking around the small area in back. Even in baggy jeans and an oversize shirt, her body excited him. He was losing his grip.

When horns blared, he realized he'd drifted toward the left lane. Cursing under his breath, he eased back to the right.

"Hey! I thought you wanted me to be careful." Laughing, Kip returned to her seat, buckling herself in.

"Sorry, Kip, that was stupid."

"Daydreaming?"

He grinned. "I was watching you in the rearview mirror. You're a very lovely woman . . . and very distracting."

She shook her head. "You're crazy." Yet she couldn't deny the pull he exerted on her.

Mouth twisted in a wry smile, he nodded. "I've come to the same conclusion, but it doesn't help." He grimaced at her. "I may have to marry you."

"Well, don't bend your brain over it. There's no chance," she shot back.

"Then you marry me."

"Same thing," she mumbled, unable to keep from grinning. "You *are* crazy."

"Is that how you feel about us?"

"Us? I'm as annoyed as you by this . . . this . . . ridiculous, silly nonsense," she finished in a rush.

"What's the solution?"

"I'm not the answer man. You figure it out."

He laughed, loving her tart tongue. She made him happy as no one ever had. And that thrilled him more than the ever-growing desire he felt for her.

"You do agree it's nonsense, don't you?" she asked. Why was she holding her breath? she wondered.

"No, I don't. I have some feelings I don't understand, but they are not silly. They're very real."

"Asinine," she muttered.

"You sound frustrated."

"Now don't try to lay that one on me. I'm not suffering from frustration, and even if I were, I wouldn't need you to handle it for me." Despite her words, the idea of making love with Bear made her insides tremble. He had it all, charm, sexiness, good looks. But what attracted her to him the most was his gentleness. She remembered the cat and dog. "How are Clancy and Dyna?"

"Fine. But we were talking about frustrations."

"I don't have any." Liar! she accused herself. Since meeting him she'd had more than a few restless nights.

"Then you handle mine," he said, and the thought of that nearly had him pulling off the road right then. He wanted her more than he'd ever wanted anything . . . yet his need to protect her and also preserve her independence went much deeper.

"No, I won't," she said sharply. She was losing control. Damn.

"Why are you so irritated?"

"I'm not. I'm . . . annoyed."

"Same thing."

"Don't think you can drop into my life like a meteor and burn all before it. I won't let you."

"Then do something about my life."

"What?"

"Why don't we get to know each other? I'm more than willing to meet you halfway."

Laughter bubbled through her annoyance, even though she tried to stop it. "That's ridiculous."

"No, it isn't."

"Rent a person to see if you could get along?"

"Something like that."

"Silly." But, oh, how wonderful. Having him around for weeks, months, longer. The sun was suddenly blindingly bright.

The miles rolled by under the wheels.

When they entered Pennsylvania, they could still see some snow on the hills, but spring wasn't to be stopped. The trees had turned a lovely violet shade, hinting that budding would begin soon, before the leaves burst into full leaf.

When Bear pulled off the expressway onto a side road, Kip looked at him questioningly.

"There's an inn along here," he said. "I've eaten there when I've skied the area."

He liked to ski, she thought. So did she. Another snippet of information.

Bear parked in the small lot beside the restaurant, then strode around the RV to open her door for her.

"Thank you," she said.

He smiled and lifted her down, then bent to kiss her nose. Straightening, he inhaled deeply. "The air is wonderful. Cold, crisp. One day next winter we'll come up here together."

Kip had every intention of upbraiding him for talking as if their being together in several months was a foregone conclusion. When her hands came up to clasp his face, she saw the shock in his eyes that she knew was mirrored in her own. "Damn you, Kenmore." She kissed him, loving the electric pressure of his lips. "Insane," she breathed, her mouth centimeters from his.

"Tell me about it," he muttered. He brushed his lips across hers, then stepped back. "Let's eat before I decide to satisfy a different appetite right now."

Fighting back a blush, she started to retort, then stopped. How could she scold him when he'd spoken her own thoughts exactly? "Ah, yes. Let's eat."

Kip loved the country ambience of the restaurant, with ruffled curtains, smiling waitresses with mobcaps on their heads, and a dessert cart that was far too rich to be legal. The torte was at least a foot high!

They ordered casseroles of cheese, ham, and potatoes that were hot and spicy. The bread—crisp, fresh, and hot—was homemade rye. The still-warm muffins were blueberry and raspberry.

Kip sat back, dabbed at her mouth, and sighed. "Cooking like that is an art form."

"Have a dessert." Bear directed her gaze to the cart that was being replenished with fresh baked goods.

"The bakery is in the back of the kitchen. I've seen it. Clean as anything."

"Too full. But seeing those wonderful pastries makes me salivate." She looked at him regretfully. "I hate it when I have to pass up these things, but cheese and fruit will be fine for me."

Bear leaned his elbow on the table, his chin in his hand. "You don't gain weight. You're too active."

"True. I am more likely to lose than gain. How about you?" She scrutinized his muscular chest and shoulders, and was sorry she'd focused on him. Her lower body felt melty and wanting.

He shrugged. "I work out. You're incredibly beautiful, you know, but I suppose everyone says that to you."

She stared at him for a moment, then shook her head. "I'm too skinny and leggy. Marsh used to say I walked like a man."

"He's an idiot. Forget him. You move like mercury, supple with controlled force. You have a beauty that's rare . . . because it's so deep."

Giddy at the compliment, she started to laugh. "Izzat so?"

"Yes, ma'am, it is." He signaled to their waitress. "I want to get something, then we'll go."

She watched as he ordered four of the desserts to be wrapped for traveling.

He grinned at her. "We have milk in the RV fridge. These will help us through if we get hungry."

"Ummm. Good idea."

"Ready?"

She nodded, noticing as she stood how he barely looked at the bills he threw down on the table. "You should get a receipt. I always do. It makes it easier for the accountant at tax time."

"This isn't a business dinner, lady. It's been pure, unadulterated pleasure."

She could feel the blood run up into her face. "For me too."

"Thank you for that." He leaned down and kissed her cheek, then kept his arm around her as they strolled out the wide door.

With the days getting longer, the sun was still just above the horizon as they walked to the small RV. Bear stopped at the door and smiled down at her. He wanted to hold the moment, cherish it and her. "Your turn to drive, Kip," he murmured. "Fine," she whispered.

He started to lower his head to kiss her, when he saw a man striding toward them.

"Hey," the man exclaimed, "I know you. You're Honey Bear Kenmore. Wow, I saw you drive at Indy. Didn't think you'd make it out of the car that day. Boom! What an explosion." The man grinned widely. Then he frowned, his glance sliding to Kip. "You can't drive Honey Bear Kenmore, lady. He wouldn't let no woman drive him."

"Yes, I would," Bear said softly. "Have a good day."

The man walked away, muttering, "Must be crazy to let a woman drive his car."

"Will I damage your image as the great macho man if I drive?" Kip asked, smiling.

"Please don't describe me as macho. I'm not. I respect women and their abilities." It worried him that Kip might think he was one of those know-it-all males who talked down to women. He'd never been like that. But it had never mattered so much that a woman know it.

Kip smiled up at him. "That stung, did it?" she asked. Bear was such a paradox. With his dark blue eyes and nearly black hair, he looked like Tarzan, but he didn't like being thought of that way. He was rough, tough, smooth, and sophisticated, and he didn't want to be slotted as any one thing. When he was racing, his nickname had been Black Frost. Journalists had described him as icy, implacable, expressionless. But she had seen him with Clancy and Dyna. And herself.

"Yes, that stung," he said, but he was smiling. He opened the door of the RV and gestured for her to precede him. "Are you sure you want to drive?"

She reached up and touched his face as she passed him. The slight contact made her quiver. No one ever had affected her that way. "I'm fine. And it's my turn to drive."

"So it is," Bear said softly, following her into the vehicle. Buckling himself into the passenger seat, he watched as she went through the quick checks before starting. "Who taught you to drive?"

"Uncle Phineas. He always told me I could be anything in the world I wanted, except a father."

Bear chuckled. "Definitely a feminist uncle." No wonder she was so well-rounded, so serene, he mused, studying her. Kip Noble knew who she was, and her worth. Yet she'd been hurt too. There were moments of grayness in those eyes at times.

"Yes, he was a wonderful man," she said. "You would have liked him." She turned the key, letting the engine idle for a few moments while she studied the various lights on the dashboard.

"I did like him. I met him a couple of years ago at an auto show. He'd brought the mock-up of his car, and it was on display. We talked for a long time about racing and the car." Bear had no trouble calling to mind the man with the shock of white hair, keen eyes, and cherubic smile. "He was a very intelligent man, and shrewder than he looked."

Kip laughed. "Yes. Did he tell you to make him an offer?"

"No, but I did make him one. He told me to come back when the car was completed, and we'd talk then."

"And that's why you were at the test driving?" She might never have met Bear Kenmore if her uncle hadn't arranged it, she realized. But she'd met Marsh through her uncle, and that hadn't been good.

"Why are you biting your lip that way?" Bear asked. He wanted to kiss her lips, not watch her bite them.

"I was thinking that it was my uncle who introduced us, in a way," she hedged, pulling onto the road. She didn't want to discuss Marsh with him at that moment.

Bear reached out a finger and touched her ear gently. "We would have met anyway, Kip. *You* know that. So do I."

"Believe in fate, do you?" It angered her that she was blushing, and that he'd again stated what she was thinking.

He shrugged. "Call it anything you like. I know we would've met."

She kept her gaze on the road, a lacing of trepidation touching her.

They drove silently for several miles.

"Do you enjoy the business world?" Bear asked suddenly.

"What?" Kip had to shift her concentration. She'd been thinking about Bear and her reactions to him. It was all too fast, too explosive . . . and so natural. "Actually, I love the challenge. I never considered doing anything but going into business with Uncle Phineas. He was my inspiration."

"Does the fierce competition bother you?"

"At times. Some of it is not to my liking. There are people I dislike and who dislike me—"

"Impossible," Bear murmured, wishing he could lift her out of that seat and onto his lap.

She shot him a prim look. "We were having a serious discussion."

"I was serious," he murmured huskily.

"Stop that. That sexy voice isn't serious." Cars whizzed by her on the expressway, but Kip stayed cool. How was it that Bear Kenmore could disconcert her when tons of steel all around her could not?

"Love," Bear said softly, "that you can think any part of me is sexy is incredibly arousing."

"Highway. Traffic." Kip inhaled to clear the squeak from her voice. "Keep your eyes on it."

"You do that. I'll watch you."

"We should talk, get to know each other."

"Fine. What would you like to know? I have a father, a mother, and two sisters. I have a few close friends, some of whom you've met. How about you?"

Kip exhaled in relief. Keep it on an impersonal level, she told herself. That way she might be able to handle the fast pulse and shaking limbs that occurred when Bear touched her. "Well, I lost my parents while in grade school. Uncle Phineas was my only relative. He saw to it that I was well educated in the humanities and the sciences, but I think he was relieved when I said I wanted to study business as well." She smiled. "We traveled in Europe, Asia, and Africa because Uncle Phineas was an amateur anthropologist. I think he hoped to find a second Peking Man."

"My mother would've loved him," Bear said. "She's always looking for an unusual dinner guest."

Kip laughed. "He was that all right. When I was a teenager, boys were always hanging around me in the hopes Uncle Phineas would let them take a spin in his newest race car."

Memory of the test driving two weeks ago, Gunder's assertion that the car had been tampered with, descended suddenly like a black cloud. She shivered.

"Someone walk on your grave?"

She nodded. "I guess so. I was thinking about the accident the day we met. It's hard to believe someone would do that."

"Who knew you would be driving that day?"

"My crew, whom I trust. I've known most of them for years." She hesitated, thinking of Richard Granger. "You think that someone would go after me just to get the car?"

"Don't sound so surprised. That car is very well designed. It has some bugs in it, yes, but it's a driver's dream. There are people who would go to great lengths to get it."

She shook her head. "Uncle Phineas would have a hard time accepting that. And so do I." Would Bear go to great lengths to get it? No!

"Why the frown? Did you think of something?"

"I don't believe someone would try to kill me for a car," she muttered.

He turned toward her. "And that's a naive remark, considering people are being killed for the change in their pockets."

"I know, I know, but it seems trivial, meaningless to put so much value on an inanimate object and so little on people's lives." Never, never would Bear hurt her. She hadn't known him long, but she was sure of that.

"I agree, lovely lady."

He put on a tape, and the beautiful strains of a Mozart concerto filled the RV. "I hope you like this." He yawned. "Sorry. A touch of left over jet lag."

"I do like the music. Why don't you go back and lie down?"

"I'd rather sit up here with you."

Joy rippled through her, and she had to force herself to concentrate on the road and not watch him. After several minutes of silence she glanced over to see that his head had slipped to one side. His lips were slightly parted, his eyes closed. He was sleeping. She smiled and drove on.

Driving through Pennsylvania was a delight. There weren't many cars, and the scenery was starkly beautiful. As they descended out of the mountains, though, the traffic increased.

Sunset dropped into a gray sky, then darkness fell like a cloak. Headlights popped on.

"What the hell?" Bear exclaimed, waking abruptly. "Kip, pull over. I didn't mean to pass out like that. You've been driving too long. Look, there's a truck stop. Pull in there."

She was glad to pass the driving over to Bear. They were getting close to the Pennsylvania and New Jersey border. From there it would be very heavy driving into Manhattan.

They both got out of the vehicle to stretch their legs and use the bathrooms. Bear waited for her outside the ladies' room, taking her arm as they walked back to the RV. "You're tired. I can feel your arm quivering."

"I am a little, but I liked driving. I always have."

"So have I."

His teeth flashed in a smile, and Kip's heart turned over. When he leaned down, his hands sliding around her, she didn't pull back. It would have been sensible to do so. Instead she lifted her arms and locked her hands behind his head. "A couple of drivers, that's us."

"You sound out of breath." His lips were inches from hers.

"And you sound like you've got a sore throat."

"You have that effect on me, love. You take my breath away, as the song says."

"You like music, do you?" she whispered, noticing how the lights of the rest stop flashed over his tough face, a face that had become familiar, dear, comfortable. He made her blood boil, but she felt serene with him. What would it be like to be with him all the time? Desire swept through her, and she forced it away. She'd read enough about the Kenmore family to know they were wealthy and moved in a lofty social strata. It wasn't one she expected to join. And after her unhappy experience with marriage, she had vowed to be especially cautious with men.

"I like you, Kip Noble," Bear murmured. Then he kissed her, gently, sweetly, urgently. Her heart beat out of rhythm. Blood pounded through her veins. For a moment she allowed herself to need him.

Four

Bear stayed late when they arrived at Kip's apartment, helping her organize her things. The apartment had been her Uncle Phineas's, and she had been using it for the past year when she commuted.

After she was satisfied with the unpacking, they had coffee, sitting on the couch. When Bear took the cup from her and enfolded her in his arms, she went willingly, her hands exploring him. Soon they were lying down, she on top of him, their mouths open and eager, their hands urgent and questing. Desire swiftly rose toward a crescendo. Kip struggled to hang on to her sanity, but the wonder of touching Bear was overwhelming her.

The phone rang. Shaken, she stared at it.

"Ignore it," Bear said.

She shook her head and sat up to answer it.

"Hello? Oh, Marsh. Hello." She looked at her watch. What was he doing calling so late? For that matter, why was he calling at all? "Yes, I got here fine," she answered him. "Thanks for your concern. Good-bye."

She hung up and turned to Bear. All signs of passion were gone. His eyes were cold, unreadable.

Kip stared at Bear when she hung up the receiver. "I should get some sleep," she said awkwardly, rebuttoning her shirt. "I have a long day tomorrow."

"Of course."

They'd said good night stiltedly, yet Bear arrived at her door at eight the next morning, bearing sweet rolls and coffee. The sweet rolls were forgotten when he leaned over and kissed her. "I was a jerk last night."

"So was I," she said breathily.

He drove her to work in his Ferrari, and when he stopped in front of her office building on Fifth Avenue, they kissed over and over again. When she finally left him and took the elevator up to the third floor, she was reeling. As she started into her office, her secretary, Myrtle Weeks, stared at her face, and she hurried to the ladies' room to repair her makeup.

All through the day Bear's face was in front of her as she worked. They had dinner that night in a quiet French restaurant. They held hands and hardly noticed what they ate.

Day after day they saw each other. They always had breakfast together, either in her apartment or her office. Sometimes they found the time for a quick lunch, then they would meet for dinner. Sometimes they went to a show, but most often they preferred just to be together, holding hands, kissing, and talking about themselves.

Bear told her about growing up in a wealthy, eccentric family, about his wild times in college and afterward, when he and Piers seemed to be forever finding trouble. He talked little about racing, still not willing to share those demons with her.

Kip told him more about her uncle, the unique experiences she shared with him running his businesses, his inventions, and his traveling.

They talked about their beliefs, their likes and dislikes, their fears and their dreams. The more they talked, the more they realized how much they liked each other.

And the more they kissed, the more they realized the potent force of their attraction.

Kip felt as though a bomb were ticking inside her. Each time Bear left her, she wondered how long it would be before she begged him to make love to her.

Bear had to fight to concentrate each day, for Kip was constantly on his mind. Only the need to give her space restrained his fierce need for her. Though she hadn't said much about her marriage, that she'd been disillusioned with it was obvious. He wanted everything to be strong and sure between them, wanted her to be certain she wasn't making a mistake again.

Manhattan was a strange place to work, Kip thought for perhaps the hundredth time as she strode along Fifth Avenue one sunshiny morning, heading for her office.

As she gazed up at the clear blue sky and inhaled the sharp air of the late April day, she couldn't believe she'd been in Manhattan for three weeks. Uncle Phineas would have liked that. He'd always pushed for her to come to New York.

And each day she'd seen Bear. She was happy! She wanted to jump, dance, and sing. In Manhattan maybe no one would notice. She was unsettled that whenever she envisioned her future, Bear was always in the picture. But she couldn't blind herself to the fact that he had blotted any other man from her mind.

Crossing the street, she entered a large office building a few blocks south of some of the best stores in the country.

Morningstar Fabrics had the entire third floor, and Kip stepped out of the elevator and into the hustle and bustle of the outer office. She smiled at the staff and strode between desks to the short corridor that led to her private office.

Myrtle looked up, beaming. "He's in there," she breathed, gesturing with her head toward the closed door. "He brought breakfast. Gosh, he is beautiful, Miss Noble."

Kip felt a burning desire to remove the glass of water from Myrtle's hand and tip it over her head. That was stupid! She was jealous? Over a simple remark? Never. "I'm sure Mr. Kenmore would be pleased with your perception of him," she said stiffly.

"Do you have a headache, Miss Noble?" Myrtle looked concerned.

"Ah, no, it's nothing." Kip smiled weakly and opened her office door. He was standing with his back to her. Damn him for being a hunk, she thought. The mere sight of him made her breathing ragged and turned her knees to water. And just because she'd looked at him! Kissing him was a little death. She stepped over the threshold and shut the door. It closed with an almost inaudible thud.

Bear, it seemed, was too busy to notice her. He'd made a space on her desk and was arranging cups, cutlery, and napkins.

"Hi," she said coolly, wanting to throw herself into his arms.

Bear turned, almost upsetting one of the cups. "Hi, yourself." He strode over to her and took her in his arms, kissing her gently. His heart thudded against his breastbone; his body hardened. Three weeks of being with her most of the time had made him want more. She was in his dreams at night, his thoughts during the day.

He released her and studied her, loving the somnolent look in her eyes, the sensuous droop to her mouth. "Whatever you're thinking," he murmured, "it must be wonderful. You're so beautiful, so womanly, Kip."

His desire for her galloped through him. No one had ever reached inside him as she had. It was as though she'd peeled away every layer and found facets of him that even he hadn't known were there. Love was not a word he'd dealt with very often, or easily. He loved his friends; he loved some of his relatives. With Kip he always wanted more, needed to be closer. He'd discovered that he wanted to cherish, and be cherished, that he wanted years, not just moments.

It was tough to be patient. He had to fight the urge to carry her off to a desert island and make love to her for three days straight. But Kip had to want it that badly too.

"I was thinking that I'm hungry," she said, not adding that she was hungry for him. "What have you got?"

"You'll like it." He led her to the desk, his hand resting lightly at her waist.

"Where did you get the hot plate?" She shook her head. "And toaster?"

"The store, of course. See, we have hot rice bran, whole-wheat English muffins, and grapefruit slices." He pulled out her chair and edged another one close to it for himself. Shaking out her napkin with a flourish, he laid it across her lap and began ladling cereal into a bowl.

"Enough, enough," she said, laughing. She'd never felt so warm, so cared for. It was an unlooked for and unique experience.

Living most of her life with a loving yet occasionally absentminded uncle had not prepared her for world-class cherishing. Marsh Finewood had been smooth. He hadn't been a cherisher. "This is fun."

Bear leaned over and kissed her lightly. "Why does your shy smile arouse me?"

She choked on her orange juice. "You're outrageous." Everything about him aroused her.

"Not me."

"Yes, you. You say those things to disconcert me, you monster." She struggled to keep the smile off her face, but she couldn't. His company was having its usual profound effect on her. She couldn't recall ever being so happy, or even considering she could be. Though she'd never thought of herself as unhappy, happiness had not been a word she'd related to herself. Busy, committed, eager to see friends, more than a little ambitious. But happy? That was a new word.

"I'm not trying to disconcert you," Bear said softly, tucking a tendril of hair that had come loose from her chignon. "I'm just being honest."

She turned to him, her lips parted in a loving smile, but her intercom buzzed abruptly. He glared at it as she pressed the button. "Yes, Myrtle?"

"Mr. Finewood is on line two, Miss Noble."

"Oh. I forgot to return his call yesterday. Could you tell him I'll call him back in about an hour?"

"Does he call often?" Bear asked sharply as she released the button.

Kip stiffened. At that moment she could have killed him for destroying the moment. "People call here all the time," she said tightly.

He clenched his fists to stop himself from hurling the phone across the room.

"Finewood isn't just anybody. He's your ex-husband."

"I know who he is."

The camaraderie had evaporated. In its place was a heavy silence filled with frustration.

"Marsh's business," she went on, "is having a special showing and sale this week. I said I'd go." Dammit, she didn't need to explain anything to him. Damn him for being mad at her!

"Of course. When is the sale?"

Kip was glad to look away from him as she reached for her calendar. She flipped the pages, noticing that her hand was shaking. "Friday."

"Umm, sounds interesting."

"Actually, it will be. The rugs they import from the Mideast and Far East are usually exceptional, and, of course, all handcrafted."

"Of course."

"That's why Marsh was trying to buy Morningstar Textiles five years ago, to expand their market."

"And that's when your uncle met him?"

She nodded. "Then he brought him home to dinner, and I met him." Why was she going over past history with him?

Bear nodded slowly, even as every nerve in his body hated what she was telling him. To hell with Finewood! He pushed back his chair. "I should go or we'll both be late getting started."

Kip stood as well. "Yes." The barriers that had been thrown up with Marsh's call were still too high. She wanted to burst through them and throw herself into his arms, but she said and did nothing.

Bear kissed her cheek, then turned and strode to the door. With his hand on the knob, he stopped and stalked back to her, sweeping her into his arms, his mouth finding hers as though it were his life force.

Her lips parted beneath his as her arms slid around his waist, clutching at him, keeping him close.

The kiss went on, sealing them together, making them one.

Bear's arms convulsed around her, folding her tight to him. He didn't know who groaned, but his blood pounded through his veins, his heart thudded against his ribs. She was pulling him apart . . . and he wanted it that way!

Kip would have fallen if he hadn't been holding her. She was turning to soft wax, and Bear was remolding her with a love that had her breathless.

They couldn't get enough of each other. Passion whirled them away, and it was only the sound of her intercom buzzing again that kept them on earth.

Bear put her from him, noting that her face was pale, her mouth trembling. He started to speak, then swung around and strode from the room. He'd wanted to make love to her right in her office, for God's sake.

Kip reached out a hand to stop him, then let it fall to her side. The silence was thunderous after his departure. She felt as though her body had left her to go with him. He had at least taken all of her zest and vitality, leaving a void. Bear. Bear. She'd wanted him to love her. If he'd suggested they do it on the desk, she would have gone along with him, she thought dazedly.

Looking around her, she blinked. Myrtle must have given up, because her intercom had stopped buzzing.

Shaking her head to clear it, she sat down at her desk and spotted the phone message from the day before about Marsh. Might as well get it over with, she thought, and dialed his number.

His secretary put her through immediately.

"Hi, Kip. I just wanted to remind you of the sale on Friday."

"I hadn't forgotten." But she didn't feel like going. She had enough work to keep her busy for a month. Besides, Marsh made her uncomfortable. Every time she saw him she wondered how she could have married him. They didn't suit each other at all. She didn't need to be reminded of her stupidity. "I'll be there, but I can't stay long."

"Once we get you here, I hope to change your mind."

"Sorry, Marsh, I can stay an hour, no more." Even that would put her behind. If she was going to spend time away from her work, she'd prefer to be with Bear.

"All right, Kip. You know, I still can't believe you left Detroit. You loved it there. You might be sorry."

"Maybe." Sorry? she thought. With Bear in Manhattan? Not likely.

Friday was crisp, cool, and damp. The sky had a leaden hue, as though it were weighted down with moisture. People scurried from taxi to building, or scuttled down the sidewalks.

Kip looked up at the modest facade of Finewood and Son's Madison Avenue store and showroom, and smothered a sigh. Best to go in and get it over with. She hadn't seen Marsh's family since the divorce, and she didn't miss them. Though she'd never had a problem with his family, they didn't appeal to her.

She pushed open the door, and her brows rose. The Finewoods were doing well if the salesroom was any measure of their success. It was bigger, more opulent, and everything looked brand new, except for the carpets, which were richly glowing antiques. She wondered if Marsh's return to the business had anything to do with this new wealth.

The only person in the salesroom directed her to the

back of the store, and she paused on the threshold of the spacious showroom. People were standing, sitting, chatting in clusters, and gazing at the richly displayed rugs everywhere in the room.

"There you are, darling," Marsh said warmly, coming up to her. "I've been looking for you."

He bent his head, but Kip turned her face so that the kiss landed on her cheek instead of her lips. "Back off, Marsh." She smiled tightly. "We've been divorced for more than three years, and we were glad to part."

He shrugged. "I was perfectly willing to carry on with our marriage."

"With all your mistresses in tow, it would have made quite a caravan." Her smile widened. "Don't frown. Show me some rugs." She turned toward one of the displays. "Umm, these are new. Peruvian, aren't they?"

"Yes. I didn't know you were still interested in South American art." Marsh lifted the heavy llama-wool floor covering. "This catch your fancy? Of course, you'd get the family discount."

"No discount, Marsh. If I see something I want, I'll pay full retail."

"Still too independent." He took her arm and led her across the crowded room, smiling and speaking to staff and guests, but not pausing. "I have new rugs from Iran. Of course, they come to us from Turkey." He stopped in front of a bar of Persian rugs, with cream, pale green, pink, and blue backgrounds. "What do you think?"

"Kermans. My favorite. They must cost the earth."

"They do. Choose one." He lifted a rug. "By the way, if you're in the market to sell Morningstar Textiles, I'd be interested. As you can see, we've been expanding, and we have to have more room. If I could use Morningstar's showrooms and factory for storage, it would be perfect for us."

She didn't answer as she studied him. Many women would call him handsome. She'd once thought so. Tall and slender, with dark blond hair and deep brown eyes. Perhaps if she'd never met Bear Kenmore she might still have thought him attractive.

"Why are you smiling?" he asked.

"Because I have the feeling that you invited me here so you could talk me into selling Morningstar."

He grinned. "Not altogether, darling. I wanted you to see the rugs. And that's the truth."

"I am glad I came." She turned and fingered the creamy Kerman. "I like this one." She looked for a tag. "What's the price?"

"I'll give it to you, if you sell me Morningstar. I'm desperate for space, and that's close to us. What do you say?"

She shook her head. "I'll take the smaller Kerman and the two Sarouks."

"I'll buy it," a man said suddenly.

Kip gasped. "Bear! What are you doing here?"

"I came to buy you a rug as an engagement present," he said icily.

"As a what?" She stared at him agog. She had the feeling she was seeing the man called Black Frost, not the Bear Kenmore she knew.

"You never said you were getting married, Kip," Marsh said.

"No kidding," she muttered, feeling the blood run up her face. Bear was being damned high-handed. And it was no end of annoyance to her that her body was trembling with delight. Marriage! That word took on new luster with Bear.

"We've kept it a secret until now," he said. "I'll take this one and that one. Are you ready to go, Kip?"

"I don't think we've met. My name's Marsh Finewood. And you are?" Marsh's aristocratic features were tight.

"Bear Kenmore, Kip's fiancé," Bear said tautly.

"Now, listen—" Kip began. Bear wasn't going to ride roughshod over her . . . even if the thought of being his wife delighted her.

"It's a very nice show," Bear interrupted her. "Let's go, *darling.*" He correctly read the signs when she curled up her fist, and he gripped her upper arm.

"Wait, Kip," Marsh said as Bear started to steer her through the crowds. "We were talking."

"Have to go, Marsh. Liked the rugs." She glared at the man pulling her across the room. "Let me go. This is ridiculous."

"You'll crack the enamel on your teeth if you clamp them that way." Bear was regaining his equilibrium the more space he put between Finewood and himself. "I know you don't like this. And believe me, this is a first for me—"

"How dare you troll me across the room like a fish on a line!" She tried to jerk her arm free, to no avail.

"We're leaving. Unless you'd like a glass of punch. And I'm not letting go of you because you're liable to take a swing at me."

"You've got that right. I'd like to punch you right in the nose, that's what I'd like," she said through her teeth.

"I know. That's why I'm holding your right arm."

"I'm ambidexterous." She saw one of Marsh's cousins staring at her, eyebrows raised. She smiled weakly as they sailed past him. "People are staring," she muttered.

"That's not surprising. You're a very attractive woman."

"That's not what I meant, and you know it."

Bear pushed open the door and led her out to the street. "If I said I'm sorry and that I had no intention of dragging you out of there, would that help?" He felt like carting her to Tahiti and making love to her for a year straight.

"No, it wouldn't. I don't like high-handed tactics, yours or anyone else's." But through the anger there was the heat that his words had evoked, and that was almost more irritating than his actions.

"I don't like them either," he said. "Damn, I just hated how intimate and friendly you and Finewood looked."

"What?" She'd been eager to get away from Marsh.

"My car's over there."

"I hope you have a ticket."

"Phelps is driving. I won't." Bear opened the door and ushered her into the plush interior of the Rolls.

"Hello, Phelps." She shook free of Bear's hold and slid across the richly upholstered seat.

"You sound angry, Kip."

"That doesn't even describe it," Bear said. "She was going to wallop me in front of a great many people."

"About time she took you down to size." Phelps was still laughing when Bear pressed the button to raise the window between the front and back seat.

Kip turned to face Bear. "What were you doing at the sale?"

"Buying a rug."

"And telling Marsh we were engaged. Why did you do that?"

"It was either that or smack him one." His eyes hardened. "Where does he get off calling you darling?"

"It's none of your business. Besides, he calls everyone darling."

"You're divorced!" Bear's thundering reply echoed.

"I know that. Don't you raise your voice at me, you—you twit."

Phelps's shoulders hunched over and shook.

"Dammit, Phelps," Bear shouted. "You turn off that speaker."

"Stop bellowing," Kip said. "I'm the one who was humiliated. How dare you say we're engaged?"

"If he can call you darling, I can say we're engaged," Bear shot back.

She shook her head. "You sound like a child."

He scowled at her, then subsided in his corner. "I know. Dammit, he made me mad." He slouched down farther when she laughed. "Very funny."

"It is. Better grow up, little boy."

"I am grown up." He looked at her. "Sorry. I had no intention of making a scene when I went in there."

Still chuckling, Kip took hold of his hand. "I like the rugs you bought. I hope you know they'll set you back a huge amount."

"I'd like to give them to you." When Kip would have withdrawn her hand, Bear tightened his. "As a gift from a friend to a friend." He kissed her palm. "I don't know what's building between us, Kip, but I know I like seeing you for breakfast, lunch, and dinner. What do you like?" He kissed her eyes, her lips, her hair, his mouth lingering.

"Well, I don't see you during my coffee break," she said breathily. She moved back a bit. "Put your rugs in your place, Bear, just for now."

He stared at her for a moment, then nodded.

Her hands had a life of their own as they curled into his hair, tugging gently to bring his mouth to hers.

Feelings exploded at once, and she groaned against his lips, wanting him. Planets and stars whirled behind her eyes, and her desire climbed. Pressing tightly to him, she sighed her longing. Happiness bubbled through her. Passion was hot and melting.

Bear felt all his barriers disintegrate. The need to give himself to her, to have her, to love her, overflowed. Black ice turned to hot lava because of Kip. His mouth slanted over hers, his tongue intruding, touching hers.

Had she just burned her bridges? Kip wondered as her tongue jousted with his.

Then, like a pail of cold water, reality flooded over her, and she pulled back.

"We have to go slow, Bear. I married on impulse once, and I knew it was a disaster the first week. We were divorced before our first anniversary." It took all of her will not to dissolve in his arms again.

"I'm willing to invest some time in us," he said. "How about you?" All of his preconceived notions about how it would feel to be in love had blown apart with Kip. He belonged to her, whatever she decided.

"I'll give it a shot," she said. Committing herself to him, even in such a small way made her heart beat out of rhythm.

"Shall we go to a show tonight?" He kissed her fingers.

"Actually, I thought I'd fix dinner. I'll make a spaghetti carbonara you'd die for, and I've got a pouilly-fuissé that has just the right tartness to go with it."

"I'll bring garlic bread."

"Come early and help with the salad."

Spontaneously they clasped hands and smiled at each other. The world had righted itself.

When Phelps stopped the car in front of Morningstar, Bear walked her to the door, kissed her, shot a glance at the building, then looked at her quizzically.

"What is it?"

"Do you think you'll sell your business to Finewood?"

"So you heard that." She sighed. "No, I don't want to sell. I make a good living out of the textile business." She frowned. "I told you a man named Richard Granger tried to buy me out, and if I can resist his high-pressure tactics, I think I can handle Marsh."

"Tell me more about this Granger."

She shrugged. "I don't think I need to now. He seems to have backed off. At least I haven't heard from him in a while." She grinned. "I'm surprised that Marsh didn't ask for the car. He always loved fast cars."

"Maybe his offer for Morningstar is a red herring."

She laughed. "Not everyone's as devious as you. See you later." She kissed him, disappeared inside the building.

Bear stared after her for long moments, his hand on his lips. Lightning had just struck him on Fifth Avenue.

Strolling back to the car, he got into the front seat and sank back against the cushions.

"Piers said you were hit bad," Phelps said. "Now, I believe him."

"She's wonderful, isn't she?"

"Yeah." Phelps shot him a quick glance. "But not everybody thinks so. Gunder says that race car of hers had been tampered with by a professional."

Bear nodded, his face hardening into lines of granite. "I'm working on the premise that it's one of those fly-by-night racing outfits that wants a jazzy car for promotion."

"It's weak, and you know it." Bear's smile turned to sculpted steel. "Don't kill anybody, Bear."

"That all depends on what I find." And if anyone was menacing Kip . . . Anger pulsed through him. He would take care of her.

"You don't really believe it's a fly-by-night outfit," Phelps said.

"Tell me where else to start."

Phelps shook his head. "I don't know. I don't think Kip feels she has an enemy."

"True."

"And maybe she doesn't, but you have plenty."

Bear nodded. "If anybody is coming at me through her . . ."

"Easy, Bear. Either way you could take a dive. You don't want to get hurt, and you don't want her to catch one either."

"Right. I've called Shim Locke. He'll look into her background. Maybe her uncle had an enemy."

"I thought he was out in California with Dolph for the indoor shooting of his picture."

"He is. But he'll either send one of his people or delegate someone to Dolph and come himself."

"You've always said he was good. I'd like to meet this guy who guards Dolph."

Bear nodded. "I've only met him a couple of times myself, but Dolph says he's top drawer." Bear smiled, recalling another time. "And he handled something for Piers and Damiene."

"Yeah, I heard about that. But he's with Dolph most of the time, right?"

"Yes. Not that the big man likes to be guarded."

"It does seem kind of funny to have someone watch Dolph. He's as tough as you." Phelps sent him a worried glance. "But it wouldn't hurt if he took a look at things. Gunder and I can keep our eyes open, but . . ." He shrugged expressively.

"Even when he comes, that doesn't mean we let down our guard."

"No way, Bear. You know us."

"I do. Thanks."

• • • •

Three days later Kip was wandering around her apartment, flipping through some of her uncle's books, touching the chair in his study. "Uncle Phineas, I wish you were here. I need your advice." She was definitely going to be certified, she thought. Talking to herself! What next?

The apartment wasn't really spacious, and the rooms were small so that she covered the entire area several times while she tried to come to grips with her dilemma. Bear Kenmore!

They were going to Little Italy that evening for dinner. Though they saw each other constantly, the rhythm was easy. Bear wasn't pressuring her. Then why did she feel crowded, threatened?

Examining her own feelings became too uncomfortable, and she fled to the bathroom. A cold shower might chase the uneasy feelings away.

It was hard to admit that she'd reached a plateau where it was difficult for her to hold back. She wanted Bear and she needed him. That scared her.

How had he gotten past her guard? After the fiasco with Marsh, she'd vowed never to get involved again. Almost from the beginning she'd realized she had made a mistake marrying Marsh. She didn't love him. After a time she found some of his principles questionable, and there'd been a loss of respect. But she'd been determined to see it through—until she'd discovered Marsh was playing fast and loose with her emotions. While pretending to love her, he'd been seeing an assortment of women. It had been a relief to face him about it.

"Since you need to indulge in those sorts of games," she'd told him the evening she'd flown to New York for a surprise visit, "and since I don't think it wise or healthy to be unfaithful, I'm leaving you, Marsh."

"Now, Kip, wait a minute. Give the marriage a chance. We've never even had a fight. Most people don't have that."

"I've given it ten months of faithfulness, you've given it nothing. I'm not angry, Marsh, but I want out. Don't buck me on this. You feel very constricted in this marriage anyway. Admit that."

He hadn't answered her, but he'd put no barriers in the way of the divorce.

Kip had put the marriage behind her with the greatest relief, vowing never to become so emotionally caught up in another relationship that she lost her good sense.

She figured she'd be attracted to someone else eventually, would want to be with that person. But everything would be in writing. She'd take cool, legal steps.

With Bear it was a hurricane. She was bound to him without words, without law, without anything but . . . love.

Damn. She'd kept that hidden in her being. Yet Bear was in her mind night and day. Happiness was a flood in her when they were together. Was she losing control?

Getting out of the shower, she dried her hair and body, mulling the future, unable to picture it without a tall, dark-haired, blue-eyed man in it.

That evening Bear picked her up early. She directed him to the small study to wait for her.

At first he just glanced cursorily at the books on the shelf. When he became aware that there were many first editions and rare books, he became totally engrossed. And the journals!

Kip found him slouched down in her uncle's worn leather chair, a book in his hand. Watching him sent pleasure coursing through her. His expression of such concentration gave him a vulnerable air, a boyish look. She wanted to hug him, cuddle him, care for him— even though no man on earth had ever been more capable of taking care of himself. Besides, he'd hate being cosseted. She couldn't help that, though. She could scarcely stem the urge to wrap her arms around him and croon to him. She was definitely coming apart at the seams.

"Hi," she said.

"Umm?" Bear looked up slowly; then the vagueness slipped away, and he placed the book on the desk. "Hi. You look wonderful in satin." He walked over to her and took her hands; then he bent down and kissed her at the corner of her mouth. "That gold-and-platinum hair is wonderful. Turquoise is beautiful on you."

"Thank you." No sense telling him she'd gone through almost her whole wardrobe before she decided on the first outfit she'd pulled from the closet—a pencil-straight skirt and high-necked blouse, both in turquoise satin.

Her heart beating erratically, she reached up and touched his cheek. "I hate to think what I'd get if I wore a ball gown."

"Mind-boggling, isn't it?" He kissed her ear, letting his tongue trace the curve.

"Yes." Eyes closing, she swayed into him for a moment. Then she pushed back and looked up at him. "No vacillating. You have to feed me, I'm hungry."

"All right. I'm hungry too." He didn't hold back. He couldn't. Bear knew his eyes were telling her just what he hungered for, and who could satisfy that hunger.

"That's illegal," Kip whispered. "If it isn't, it should be."

"It's not, it's real," he whispered, pressing his body against hers.

"Bear Kenmore, we're both hungry for food. Let's

go." She grabbed his hand, knocking the book he'd been reading onto the floor. "Oh. What are you reading?"

"Something I shouldn't, I suppose. It's a diary of your uncle's, I think."

She laughed. "He was religious about his journals. He believed that every minute was precious, and so he'd put down his thoughts before he retired at night." She waved her arm at the shelves. "If you want to read them all, you're welcome to them."

He stared at the floor-to-ceiling bookcases. "You're not serious."

"Oh, but I am. My uncle was an inveterate diarist and journal keeper. I'll bet I could find out more about Africa by reading his journals than an encyclopedia. He loved that continent and did extensive traveling there. And, as I told you, he was also an amatuer anthropologist."

Bear shook his head. "What a man. You're proud of him, aren't you?"

"Oh, yes, and I miss him yet. His death was so sudden, and he'd never had heart trouble. The doctors said he died in his sleep, so they don't think he suffered. But it was very hard for me to take. It's been over a year, yet the shock is still with me." She tried to smile. "My uncle and I had been planning a trip together to Kenya when it happened. Of course I didn't go. I wanted to see Africa with his perception, not alone." Tears sprang into her eyes. "Sorry. I don't mean to be teary. It's stupid."

Bear took her in his arms. "It's never stupid to love someone, to miss them when they're gone. He was your family." He kissed her gently, wanting to be her buttress against pain and grief.

"Yes. And he was a wonderful father and mother, sister and brother. I never had anyone else, and I was never lonely while Uncle Phineas was alive." And she hadn't been lonely since Bear had come into her life. But he'd brought more than comfort. He'd given her passion along with cherishing.

He lifted her chin. "I'd like to be your family."

She blinked at him, shaking her head slowly. "I can't kid about something like that."

"And neither can I." Bear tightened his hold on her. "I'm very serious, Kip. I told you we'd go slow, and we've seen each other every day, talked, and gotten to know each other." He stroked her cheek. "I know you better than anyone in the world, and you know me."

Barely breathing, she stared up at him. "What are you saying?"

"I want to marry you. Will you be my wife?"

Five

Little Italy was almost a total waste of time to Kip. She saw it, she ate there, she loved her pasta, her espresso, her cannoli for dessert. But she was in a fantasy. Wasn't it a fantasy? No matter how she argued with herself, she couldn't change the river of joy that thundered through her.

"Kip?"

"Umm?"

"Look at me."

"Why?"

"Because you haven't really looked at me since I proposed to you. And more importantly, you haven't answered." And never had words mattered so much.

"I thought you were joking," she muttered, staring up at a beautiful brick house. "Wonderful architecture."

"Kip, look at me."

Dragging her gaze from the building, she forced herself to meet Bear's eyes. "All right, I'm looking."

"You know I wasn't joking because I told you I was serious."

"Yes, you did, but I was peering below the surface, peeling back the layers."

Bear took hold of her upper arms. "You can peel until you get to my skeleton. It won't change things. Kip, we're good together. You can see that."

She nodded. "But I married once, and it was a disaster."

"Dammit, don't compare us to another time. There's no comparison."

"Yes, there is." She wanted to cave in, to melt in his arms. Caution, born of scarring, held her back. "Marriage changes things."

Bear sucked in a furious breath and released her. "Okay. You have a right to take this in small steps. I don't agree with you, but I'll go along with it." He looked around him, studied the shops, the private dwellings with their lacy iron grillwork. Then he looked down at her. "Fine. We don't talk about marriage right away. We could live together for a time and see how things go. Would that suit you?"

Kip's mind went blank. Live with Bear! Delight fragmented her thoughts. But recalling how she catapulted into marriage once was like a slap in the face. "Let me . . . let me think about it." She saw the hurt flash through his eyes and put her hand up to him. He stepped back from her, his face a mask.

"Do that. And let me know," he said tightly. He couldn't remember it ever mattering to him if a woman turned him down or accepted him. A firm belief in female and male autonomy had always been a part of him. Yet Kip had lacerated him by hedging. The thought that she didn't want him as much as he wanted her was like a sword slicing through him.

"Tomorrow at the latest," she said, although she knew already. She wanted to live with him. But it was better to wait, to drag out her little fears one by one and examine them. Fidelity, trust, integrity were just words until applied to a relationship. Then they became ways of life. She had to think it through.

That she cared deeply for Bear was a certainty, and she accepted that she wanted him. But he'd mentioned marriage before he mentioned living together, and that stuck in her mind. Marriage was another story. That had to be mulled over long and hard. There was still scar tissue on her mind and soul from the first time. Though she trusted and cared about Bear more than she'd even conceived of when she'd been with Marsh, there were serious doubts that she'd have to deal with before she considered marriage. That saddened her, because, in all honesty, she wanted to scoop Bear into her arms and run to the nearest minister or judge and tie the knot. And that was scary.

When they continued their stroll, Bear no longer held her hand.

Kip wanted to explain, but the words wouldn't come.

It was a relief to get into the taxi for the trip home. Kip was glad Phelps wasn't driving them. He would surely have noticed the strain between Bear and herself.

They were still thirty blocks from her apartment when Bear turned to her and lifted her across his lap. "Will you forgive me for being a jerk, Kip? I was rushing you. You take all the time in the world to answer." He kissed her, his mouth worrying hers in questing sweetness.

She clung to him, her lips parting for him, her eyes closed. They were alone on the planet, and he was hers! Slanting her mouth across his, she gave him a more intimate access. When he groaned, her heart pounded.

Bear pulled back from her, his breathing ragged.

"Lord, angel, don't wriggle like that. I'll embarrass myself."

Her laugh was shaky as she threaded her hands through his hair. She nipped his lower lip, then ran her tongue along it. When his mouth moved over hers again, she was ready and wanting. "Bear."

"Kip, my baby."

Burying her face in his neck, Kip trembled with happiness. "I'm being a fool, I know."

"You're not. You have every right to decide how— What the hell is going on, driver?" Bear tightened his hold on her as the cab screeched to a stop. He eased Kip off his lap and leaned forward. "Are those fire trucks?"

"Yah," the driver said. "It looks like we'll have a wait if you want me to get you to the door."

"Never mind. We'll walk from here." Bear shoved some bills at him and slid out the door, turning to help Kip to the sidewalk.

"Bear, that's my place. Isn't it?"

"Looks like it. Relax, it's probably nothing. We'll talk to a fireman or a policeman." Putting his arm around her, he guided her across the street.

As they approached the yellow barriers, a policeman put up his hand.

"It's my apartment building, officer," Kip said. "Could I speak to someone, please?" She shivered, the accident with the car looming in her mind. Ridiculous, she told herself. She was being paranoid.

"Shh, it's all right," Bear said. He felt her tremble and tightened his hold on her, realizing that there must have been a sizable problem to bring so many police and firemen.

In a few minutes a fireman approached them.

"My name's Beryl Kenmore and this is Miss Noble. She lives in that building."

The fireman glanced behind him. "I don't think it'll be possible for you to stay in the building, miss. I'm afraid several of the apartments are water damaged. We were lucky no one was hurt. It seems to have started in five-twenty-seven."

She gasped. "That's my apartment."

The fireman shook his head. "The place is pretty much smoke and water damaged, miss. Do you have a place to stay?"

Shock rendered Kip speechless. Not Uncle Phineas's wonderful collection of books and artifacts. Had she been careless and left something on? No. She always checked twice before she left. But had she forgotten?

"She has a place to stay," Bear said. "Could we go up to the apartment?"

"No, sir. The place looks pretty sound, but no one will be allowed back in the building until we can be sure the fire is completely out and that the structure is safe." The fireman spread his hands. "You could call tomorrow, and we should be able to tell you more."

"Thank you. We'll do that." Bear hailed another cab and directed it to his place.

"I guess I've decided to move in with you," Kip said shakily, trying to smile.

He put his arms around her. "It's a shock when something like this happens. Tomorrow we'll get you some clothes, then we'll take a look at the place and see what can be done." He kissed her gently, then pulled back and smiled at her.

Kip stared at him. She was going to move in with him, and she didn't know the ground rules. Not even the fire took precedence over that. Her heart thudded against her breastbone as the many choices marched across her brain.

He touched her lips with one finger. "What are you thinking?"

"I hope you won't be a messy flatmate." She drew in a sharp breath. She'd be with Bear! Living with him!

He grinned. "I'll pick up." Just getting her into his home pleased the hell out of him. He kissed the corner of her mouth. "You set the pace, Kip. All the way."

She nodded, moving closer to him. "Thank you." Tears welled in her eyes. "Bear, do you think I left something on? What about my uncle's collections?"

"Don't think about it now, Kip. We'll take care of it in the morning." He kissed the top of her head. "For now, try to relax."

"All right. But you have to promise not to squeeze the middle of the toothpaste tube."

Bear laughed out loud. She'd taken a good hit when the fireman had told her about the fire and was still shook, but she was fighting back. He'd always admired courage and good planning on the track and in business. He'd never seen it manifested better than in Kip Noble. She faced what came, laid an alternate route if need be, and pushed on. "I like you, Kip Noble."

Kip looked down at her hands, amazed at the sweet sensation his words engendered in her. More than one man had professed love for her. Marsh had constantly told her he loved her. Her uncle had truly loved her and told her that often. But few men had said they liked her. Bear's sincerity had her heart beating as though he'd just professed undying love.

"Will you be my friend, Kip?"

"I think we're already there."

Bear had several good friends, some of them women. But he'd never wanted the friendship of anyone as badly as he wanted Kip's. That she had given it to him made him balloon with delight. Cherishing her in every and any way he could had become a prime force in his life. "Thank you for that."

"No. Thank you."

"How's that?" Touching her aroused him, but making her happy could give him an unexpected joy.

"You let me be myself, Bear. With you there's no artifice, nor none required. That's very relaxing." Laughter bubbled in her when he closed his eyes and groaned. "Not very macho, is it?"

"You're destroying my male ego." When her laughter built, he couldn't keep the scowl on his face. He pulled her close and pressed his face to her hair. "I'll never get a swelled head with you."

"You don't need another one," she said impishly. Though a shiver still rippled through her when she thought of the fire, she didn't feel as lost and alone as she would have if Bear hadn't been there.

"We're almost home," he said, still smiling. He saw the shadows in her eyes, but he could almost feel her rearrange herself, adjust to the new situation. Kip Noble was a gritty, gutsy lady, and he admired her greatly. More than that, having her move in with him was sending his libido flying. He wanted to sweep her into his arms and make wild love to her. But he'd promised not to push her, and he'd stick to it. Even if it killed him.

They arrived at Bear's place with a screech of brakes.

Bear paid the driver and helped her from the cab. "I think I can help out if you need any clothing for tonight."

She stiffened.

"You've got the wrong idea, Kip. One of my sisters sometimes stays with me when she comes to New York." He grimaced. "Even when I get her a reservation at a hotel, she stays with me."

Kip relaxed, smiling up at him. "What a monster you are."

"You haven't met Janine. She's insatiably curious. When I won't tell her anything, she calls Damiene and pumps her. Sometimes she even calls Dolph to see if she can get anything out of him. Piers will hang up on her if she asks too many questions."

She laughed. "That's not true."

"Yes, it is. Of course Damiene gets mad at him. She likes my sister." Bear groaned and shook his head.

"And so do you. You're just being a brother. All brothers talk about their sisters that way."

"Wait until you meet her."

On one of the middle steps Kip paused and looked up at the four-storied brownstone, its stones clean and beautiful, the wood trim around the windows fresh. "It's a quiet, lovely area."

"Yes."

The door opened before they reached it. Phelps smiled at them.

"Why aren't you in bed?" Bear asked, glaring at him.

"You're not my nanny, Bear." Phelps turned to Kip. "Howdy, lady. I hope you're going to stay awhile."

"You don't seem surprised to see us." Bear shepherded Kip into the entryway.

"One of Shim Locke's people called about the fire. He'd been watching the apartment and spotted smoke. He said he'd call back tomorrow after he talked to the fire marshal in the morning."

"Good." Bear glanced at Kip. "I was going to do that myself."

"This isn't like the car," she whispered. "I'm sure the fire was an accident."

Bear put his arms around her. "We'll know for sure tomorrow, love."

Kip saw the caring look in Phelps's eyes and her insides churned with anxiety. She pressed close to Bear, her eyes closed for a moment. The touch of a cat against her ankles had her opening them again. "Hello, Clancy."

"Listen, Kip," Bear said swiftly, "it'll be all right, I promise." Bear could have punched through a wall at that moment. He knew she was fearful, and it angered him that she should feel so threatened. He pressed his mouth to her hair. "You're still upset. You should get some sleep."

She lifted her head, trying to smile. "I'm a little tired. Maybe you could tell me which room I could use." She patted the dog, who'd come to her side.

"I put fresh sheets in the Green Room," Phelps said, ambling down a corridor to the back of the house. "See ya in the morning, Kip. You like omelets?"

"Love them."

"You'll get one after you take your vitamins, drink your juice, and eat your bran cereal." Phelps's chuckle was cut off when he shut the door.

Bear grinned when she laughed, relieved that she'd been distracted. It was time Phelps had a bonus. "You're just encouraging him when you laugh."

"I like him." She felt safe. Tomorrow she'd have to check on her uncle's things and her own, but for now she was with Bear.

"So do I."

"If you give me directions, I can find your sister's room."

"You won't be sleeping there." He took her arm and led her to the stairs. "There's a room that will be just right for you." He frowned. "And that's where Phelps put the clean sheets."

"The Green Room."

"Yes, that's what it's called, since it's mostly decorated in very pale green."

"And you're scowling because Phelps figured you'd put me there."

"Something like that," he muttered. "I'll get some clothes from Janine's room. She prefers the room on the third floor, the one you used the first time you were here."

"Do your parents come to New York?"

"Rarely. Sometimes they stay on Long Island. The family home is there, and my other sister has a house nearby. But in the last few years they've spent more time at the place in Puerto Rico. They've had it for years. They like the pace and the people. I occasionally spend Christmas with them there."

"I understand it's a beautiful island."

"Very. And the people are warm and hospitable." He led her to a room at the front of the house and pushed open the door. "I'll take you there one day. This is the Green Room." He stepped aside so that she could go into the room.

"Oh, my, this is beautiful. And that rug. Is that one of the ones you purchased from Marsh?"

"Yes. They delivered it the afternoon I bought it. I thought it would go well in here."

"It does. I like the green silk-screen wallpaper and the wainscoting. Are you your own decorator?"

"I know what I like, and I had some antiques left to me by my grandmother. A professional did the rest." He scanned her face, relishing the obvious pleasure he saw there. "I want you to be happy here and treat this as your home." It surprised him when she blushed. "Do I make you uncomfortable?"

"Maybe a little. Have you considered that you might

make me too at home?" She laughed shakily. "I might never leave."

"That would be perfect." He stared at her for a long moment, finally breaking eye contact with an effort. "I'll get the clothes."

After he left, Kip felt as though the room expanded, higher, wider, longer, and with far more oxygen. She wandered around the room, touching the precious Louis Quinze furniture. "I'm here and I want to stay," she murmured to herself, startled when her whisper seemed to echo off the high ceiling.

Tomorrow she'd try to find out about the fire. For the moment she was at peace.

Bear took the stairs to the third floor two at a time. In the guest room he rummaged through the wide closets at random, grabbing at articles of clothing that caught his fancy, dropping others. Neat most of the time, he didn't even notice the mess he was creating. Kip was in his house! It did cross his mind that Janine would have his hide for tearing through her clothes that way. What the hell!

With an armful of assorted clothing and shoes, he left the room on the run.

Rushing into Kip's bedroom, he stopped short. She was curled up on her side on the bed, her left hand under her cheek, sound asleep.

He dropped the clothes on the nearest chair and knelt beside the bed. She was like a little girl, rounded into the fetal position to protect herself. Fragile, vulnerable . . . precious. He leaned down and kissed her hair softly. There was no way he was going to disturb her.

Removing her shoes carefully, he pulled the comforter over her. When she woke, she'd be stiff and her clothes would be rumpled, but she needed the sleep.

He hung up some of Janine's clothing, put the rest in drawers, and went to his own room to shower and get ready for bed.

Taking the new novel that had been recommended to him by a friend, he settled down to read. When he'd read the same sentence five times, he threw down the book.

Donning a robe, he left his room and strode down the hall to the Green Room. Pushing the door ajar, he looked into the dimly lit room. Kip hadn't moved.

He readjusted the comforter over her, then watched her for a time. He was tired, but he was also anxious about her. Was it natural to fall asleep so fast? Maybe it was. It still made him uneasy.

Squinting in the darkened room, he fixed on the chaise longue. It was heavy, but he lifted it easily and carted it over to the bed, lowering it quietly to the floor.

It was not the most comfortable way he'd ever slept, but he was content. His anxiety wouldn't have let him sleep away from her. Since he'd met her, he'd been worried about her. Now it was part of his heartbeat to be concerned.

In short order her peaceful breathing soothed him into sleep.

When Kip woke, the gray light told her it was near daybreak. She felt constricted and oddly out of place. Gazing up at the ceiling, she stiffened. This wasn't her room. Where was she?

Lying perfectly still, she allowed the slides of memory to play back on her brain. Fire! The car! Why did those two incidents run together in her mind. Granger! No, she wouldn't let her thoughts turn that way. When the fire marshal gave his report, she'd know more. Looking around her, she inhaled shakily. She was in Bear's house. The Green Room.

Stretching made cramped muscles protest painfully. She ran her hands over her body. Good Lord, she'd fallen asleep fully dressed!

She turned onto her side and saw him at once. Bear was lying on a chaise longue, dressed in printed pajamas. The comforter he'd used had slid down his body, which was contorted to fit the confines of his makeshift bed.

Easing herself to a seated position, Kip indulged herself in a rare luxury—watching Bear sleep. She'd gotten into the habit of masking her feelings toward him in easy banter and laughter. Only when they kissed and touched did her control slip. But now there was no need to struggle for self-control. She could release the dam of sensations she experienced in his presence.

It didn't take much effort to catalogue those feelings. She cared for Bear more than she'd ever cared about anyone. And that had happened so fast.

For more days than she cared to count, she'd been looking to him as a necessary part of her daily life. How had he gotten past her barriers? It didn't matter. He'd reached into every layer of her, every crevice and curve, and it had all ballooned into a river of feeling that she shied from naming.

Gritty and mussed, she decided to shower and remove some of the grime. At the same time she noticed the small, tidy pile of underclothing on a chair and sighed with relief. Had he forgotten the other things?

Moving as quietly as she could, she rose from the bed and tiptoed to the wall-wide closets with their built-in drawers. She took out an assortment of clothing and crept to the bathroom.

Under the light she was able to discover what she'd chosen. Filmy silk underthings, tailored silk slacks and shirts. She smiled. Bear's sister was much the same size as she. Perhaps not quite as tall, but the clothes would fit.

Stepping into the shower, she closed her eyes and turned on the water. Ahhh!

Bear opened his eyes and groaned. He felt as if he'd been chained into a contortionist's pose. Muscles and sinews ached. His neck was so stiff he could hardly turn his head. Never a morning person, he closed his eyes again and rolled off the couch. Had he been reading and fallen asleep on the chaise longue? Oh, well, he'd remember eventually.

Good old Phelps had run his shower. Feeling his way, bumping his toes more than once, he cursed in a steady stream as he limped to the bathroom, his eyes still closed. It was easier to feel his way than face the day. Damn! He'd smacked his shin again. Had Phelps moved the furniture? Ah, the bathroom door.

The steam was welcome. The light was not. Bear shut his eyes more tightly. Stripping off his pajamas he slid back the door to the stall and stepped inside.

"Hey!"

"Wha . . .?" Off balance, Bear tried to turn. He bumped against another person and drew back. That was enough to knock him off his feet. Falling with a crash into the large tub that was more than big enough for two people, he struck his shoulder on a faucet. "Damn!"

To add insult to injury, someone smacked him on the top of the head with a soggy facecloth. "Wait a minute." Memory flooded back. "Kip? Is that you? Were you showering? Look, I'm sorry." Trying to scramble to his feet, he fell again.

"Oh my. I'm sorry for hitting you, Bear. I should've

known it was you. But what are you doing in my shower?" Kip leaned over to help him rise.

Bear fell back against the side of the tub, his eyes glued to the most wonderful sight he'd ever seen. "You're beautiful. I don't care if you hit me again, you're lovely."

"I'm not going to hit you." Straightening, she was unconsciously provocative when she crossed her arms in front of her."Are you hurt?"

"Yes, stabbed to the heart, Kip." He stood, his gaze still on her.

She inhaled shakily, her own gaze running over him.

For long moments they stared at each other, then Kip cleared her throat. "I've always thought that people who look other people over were being impertinent."

"Not always," he said huskily. "I want you, Kip."

"I want you too. But desire isn't the only thing two people should share." Her whole being trembled with it just the same. Had ever a man been so beautiful? Her hands itched to touch that hair-roughened chest, the black curls arrowing down to a narrow line that ended at the junction of his body. For the very first time she thought of a man's body as beautiful.

"No, but it makes a warm beginning." He reached out a hand, then let it drop to his side. He wanted to touch her, but he feared the magic in that silky, wet skin. And he'd promised her all the options.

She curled a finger into the short chest hair. "It's soft," she whispered.

"Is it?" He could barely form the words. Blood cascaded through his body, hardening it, building desire to a raging peak. "Kip?"

"I know. It's painful, isn't it? That's a surprise. I guess I've never wanted anyone enough that it hurt."

Pleasure rioted through him at her words. "Do you want me?" he asked softly.

"We're wasting water," she said feebly.

Her lopsided smile touched him like a brand. "Tell me."

"I want you, Bear. But is it smart?"

"That I don't know. I do know I want you."

She picked up the fragrant soap she'd been using. "Nothing like being clean. If you turn around, I'll wash your back."

"Fine." At the first touch his body contracted as though he'd been burned. Goose bumps erupted all over him. His lower body hardened even more. He bit his lip to stifle a groan.

Kip made damp whorls across his broad back, the rippling muscles sending her libido into overdrive. He was one wonderful piece of work. The loofah sponge slid easily over his shoulders, across the middle back, lower. His strong buttocks stiffened when she touched there. She closed her eyes for a moment and licked her lips.

"My turn," he said roughly, wheeling around and almost upsetting the two of them. If he let her continue with what she was doing, he might make a fool of himself. He wanted her too damn much.

"I'm washed and shampooed," she said out of breath. Her gaze swept over him again, and she delighted in that strong male body. "Amazing. I never thought men were beautiful before."

"And you do now?" Bear felt fatuous and foolish. Why should so much hinge on the answer to a dumb question?

"Oh, yes." Confidence poured through her. Touching one of his nipples was an urge she couldn't contain. Sure enough, it excited her. When he trembled, the feeling filled her to the exclusion of all else. What a wonderful, tingling sensation. How could it make her feel strong and weak at the same time?

"I'd better shampoo," he said.

"You have a frog in your throat, Bear Kenmore."

"And you're a siren, Kip Noble."

Bear didn't take his gaze from her as he tossed some shampoo on his head, laved it, and rinsed.

"That was fast." Kip felt lazy and warm all over.

"I was in a hurry."

"Oh? Rushing, are we?"

"Not everything." Bear could have exploded. She delighted, titillated, and aroused him. And he wanted her for a friend for all time.

"Good," she said.

"I'll dry you."

"You will?" Dreamy-eyed, Kip watched him closely. She didn't want to move, make a sound, disturb the wonderful aura that encased them.

"I will."

She let him take her hand as she stepped out of the tub. When he wrapped her in a fluffy bath sheet and began rubbing gently, she closed her eyes. "Did you hurt yourself when you fell?"

"No."

"Good." She sighed.

"Pain or ecstasy?" he whispered close to her ear.

"Both," she said huskily.

"I want to love you, Kip."

Her eyes opened, and she stared at him. "That's what living together means in one way."

"True. But it also means you can remain here, in your own room, with no one bothering you, including me." He swallowed hard. "And that means starting right now."

"Honest? Cross your heart?" Had she ever felt so energized, yet so relaxed? Happiness suffused her.

"Hope to die," he said, breathing in the fragrance of her hair as he rubbed it.

Reaching for a towel, Kip dried him slowly, stroking down his chest to his thighs. She raised her gaze to his face when his hand stopped her.

"Sorry, love. I like what you're doing, but I'm not sure I can control the immediate future if you continue."

"Oh. Can't have that. Turn around." When he did, she began the slow drying motions again. "What if I want to take this one step further?"

"Do you?"

"We're not past 'what if' yet." She patted his backside.

"Kip! Dammit, all right. We play 'what if.' " Holding himself rigid, he watched her over his shoulder, her nude body not only stirring his desire, but his protective instincts as well.

"Well, what if we shared your bed?" she asked. "Could we do it and not have sex?"

"Maybe. I'd have to spend every other hour in a cold shower."

"So would I." She thought for a moment. "We're at an impasse, I think."

"You do?"

"Yes. If we shower together and go to bed together, I think I'd want to make love together."

"I think I'd want that too." He turned around and clasped her loosely around the waist.

"There's that frog in your throat again."

"Genetic flaw?"

"No doubt. It's cute, though." She reached up and touched his chin with one finger. "There's something you should know."

"What's that?" He leaned down, wanting his body to warm her.

"I'm enjoying our game. It's not teasing with me."

"I never thought it was. Enticing is a better word."

"I'm trying to explain something."

"Go ahead." Was it hot in the bathroom, or did he have a raging fever? It didn't matter. He was happy. He liked the game too.

"You see," she said, deliberating over every word, "I didn't know that sex was fun until just now."

"Oh."

"Did you know that?"

"There are more facets to sexual play with you than I've ever imagined."

"Does that mean we've uncovered something here?"

He moved closer, his hands sliding to her hips and massaging gently. "Could be. I like it very much."

"So do I. Could it always be this way?"

"Between us there is a great possibility it could."

"I feel that way too." She smiled at him. "I don't feel like moving."

"What do you feel like doing?" He held his breath, knowing whatever answer she gave, it would be the right one for him. Kip Noble was in his blood. She made it flow, she gave him life.

Six

Kip took his hand and led him from the bathroom, her heart thudding. Not in all her life had a simple yes or no been so monumental, and she knew she would recall this time even when she was a very old woman.

They reached her bed, and Bear turned her toward him. "I want you, Kip, more than I've ever wanted anything in my life. But you should also know that you're precious to me. I want nothing to hurt you, or damage your independence, or change you one iota."

She pushed back from him, arms akimbo. "Don't try to weasel out of this assignation, Kenmore. I'll get you on breach of promise." A giggle burst from her. "Why did you close your eyes?"

"Do you know how provocative you look with your hands on your hips that way?"

Her smile became sultry. "No. Tell me, big boy." Laughter escaped her again. "I've never had such a good time. No one told me."

"No one told me, either." Chuckling, he reached for her, bringing her close to him. "Sex is a comedy routine? Do you think the idea will sell?"

"Of course. We'll market it." She kissed his throat. "I do love doing all these things."

"And there are others," he said, his hand whorling over her backside.

"Yes, I know."

She smiled at him, but Bear saw the lacing of fear in her eyes. "Kip, if I ask you a personal question, would you answer it?"

Sexual tension was replaced by stress.

"It depends." She studied him warily. "What is it?"

"Was your husband rough with you? Do you have unpleasant memories of sex?"

"That's two questions," she said faintly.

"So it is. Will you answer?"

Kip looked away from him, as though she had a need to study the intricate wainscoting. "Marsh was never rough with me, as such. But I found intercourse painful . . . and unsatisfying." She shot him a quick look. "I may be frigid." Breath whooshed out of her, as if she'd just released a tightly locked secret.

Bear shook her gently. "You're a woman of the future, Kip. You choose your mate and your lover. You're hot, loving, sensual, and determined to make that choice. Do you believe that if a man and woman love each other, and they are relatively undamaged by their pasts, there can be any coldness between them?"

"Well, yes, I do, because Marsh and I cared for each other at first, and it just didn't work."

Bear exhaled heavily. "All right. First things first." He saw a sadness in her eyes and added quickly, "Oh, I didn't mean that we wouldn't make love, Kip. I just think we should discuss some things, then love each other." He bent and lifted her easily into his arms, then carried her to the bed.

He laid her down and covered both of them, keeping

her in the crook of his arm. "Lesson number one. In order for lovers to gain satisfaction in sex, they have to strive to make their partners happy. In fact, that can be the most arousing part of it all." He kissed her nose. "Delightful foreplay, love."

She chuckled. "I'm not an unfledged girl, Bear. I know about that."

"But since you've never enjoyed it until we were in the shower, and you did enjoy that, I think we need some more schooling here."

"I will admit the foreplay in the shower was delightful." And her body had begun to heat pleasurably. That had happened at first with Marsh, but whenever there was a distraction, her body and spirit would cool. From experience she expected the coolness to deepen. With Bear it had lessened, and she could still feel some heat.

"It was delightful," Bear murmured. He leaned over her, his mouth feathering down her cheek to her neck, his strong teeth taking sensual bites of her silken skin.

Kip gasped when she felt the jab and thrust of powerful sexual heat. "My goodness."

"What is it? Have I made you uncomfortable?"

"You could say that." She looked up at him, aware that her eyes were talking to him.

"There is a little heat then." He shifted so that he was lying beside her. "Lesson number two is putting into action lesson number one."

"Oh. Then I can do this." She bit his chin, then licked the spot.

"You most certainly can." Drawing her body up his, he began kissing her breasts, his lips sliding over the satiny globes, his body boiling with the need to love and be loved.

Retaliating, she slid down so that she had access to his body. She kissed his nipples with equal fervor, her fingers curling through and tugging at the swirl of dark hair.

All at once she wanted him with an elemental need. The comparison with Marsh disappeared, and there was a deep-seated desire to give all. Torrid passion erupted in her, shocking her.

"Kip? Darling?" Bear had seen the stunned look on her face.

"Interrupting us again?" She locked her arms around him.

"Not on your life." His mouth sought hers, his hands sweeping over her soft body.

It was more than a kiss to Kip, it was an explosive sealing, a kaleidoscopic promise. Her body, mind, and soul were one, and they wanted him. There could have been roughness. Instead there was ineffable gentleness, sweetness.

When Bear's mouth moved slowly down her body, the friction of passion crackled about them, creating a force field that magnetized them. Electricity was everywhere. Each pulse point throbbed at the touch of his lips, every curve and indentation had a new life because his mouth touched there.

Ecstasy exploded in Kip, shaking her with its force. A wildness pulsed through her, stronger than anything she'd ever known, and it frightened her.

Bear felt her tremble and sensed her uncertainty, the wariness that gripped her. Tightening his hold, he caressed her lovingly, firing her as he was fired, turning her pliant in his arms.

Then he pulled away.

"What is it, Bear?"

"I'll be back. I want to take precautions with you, love."

Anger rumbled through her. She wanted no interruptions. Frustration had her passion draining away.

Bear was back in a minute, and he felt her resistance at once, how she'd cooled. "Come back to me, love." He kissed her again and again, coaxing the heat, the need, the want.

Moving slowly over her, he touched her skin everywhere. When his lips lingered on her navel, her body arched up in hot reaction.

Bear paused. Never had he felt so unsure of himself, almost giddy with delight. It was brand new, making love to Kip. Never had he wanted to give so much pleasure. Never had the merest touch given him so much joy.

"It's so great, Bear," she murmured.

He chuckled at the surprise in her voice. "Isn't it." Turning her gently, he let his mouth course down her back, his tongue lapping at the indentation of her waist, his lips sweeping smoothly over her legs to the back of her knees.

"Ooo, that's wonderful." She glanced at him over her shoulder. "I love what you're doing to me."

"So do I."

Boneless, like melting wax, she turned over so that she could clasp him around the neck. "I've never felt like this."

"Neither have I."

"Honest?"

"Yes." He slowly moved down her, his lips touching every sensitive past of her. At the joining of her body, he took her with his mouth.

Kip cried out, shock, surprise, and delight lacing the sound. Sensations exploded in her, and her low cry seemed to come from the depths of her. "I didn't know, I didn't know," she murmured over and over, as waves of ecstasy washed over her.

"Neither did I," Bear said hoarsely. Moving up her

body, he entered her gently. All thought left him as Kip empowered him with the wonderful liquid explosion of herself. He thrust into her with fierce gentleness, again and again. For the first time in his life, control left him, and he whirled gladly into the vortex that Kip had created.

"I love you, darling," he said to her as his body flew apart, then joined with hers, never to be parted again.

They held each other tightly in the throbbing aftermath, neither having the strength to talk or move.

Kip felt his gaze on her after a time and opened one of her eyes. "This is the best I can do," she told him, smiling when he chuckled.

"I'm not much better," he said softly, cuddling her against him and wiping the damp tendrils of hair from her forehead.

The one eye closed and Kip sighed, snuggling closer. "This is nice." And she trusted him.

"Yes."

"Did you tell me you loved me?"

"I did."

"Oh. I thought it might be something you say in the throes of passion."

"Not usually." He kissed her. "In fact, I've never said that to any other woman, throes or no."

Both eyes opened. "Then I suppose it's all right to tell you I love you."

He stared down at her, speechless, helpless, delighted.

"Say something."

"I'm trying," he said hoarsely.

"I told you I loved you."

"You sound morose, disgruntled about that." Happiness was a live wire in him, and he was dizzy with the knowledge that she loved him.

"Wouldn't you be?" she asked. "That phrase is tossed around so much that it sometimes has no meaning."

"I mean it."

"I mean it too, dammit." She glared at him. "But I've said it before, and it didn't work out."

"You loved your husband. I can live with that."

"Can you? Well, maybe you won't have to, because I'm beginning to think I never loved Marsh."

Bear reared up on one elbow, his other arm across her middle. "Really?"

"Well, there's no need for you to beam. I might be wrong about you too." She closed her eyes again, as though a headache had sprouted. "I would hate that."

"So would I," he murmured soothingly.

"How will I know?" Her eyes snapped open. "I'd really like to be sure."

"Live with me, and we'll get to know each other, slowly. Then we'll marry."

"You're not a realist. What if we don't suit?"

"Then we'll take an alternate route. But we will suit, I feel it."

"You're not a soothsayer. What alternate route?"

"No need to get into that, Kip." He bent down to kiss her lips. "Umm, I like your mouth . . . but then I like every part of you."

"I know. You kissed every—" She lapsed into confused silence.

"Your face is red." He laughed. "But please continue. Tell me all the places I kissed. Or I can tell you."

She tapped him on the nose. "Don't be indelicate, Mr. Kenmore."

"Umm, that prissy voice of yours is very arousing."

"Is it?" She chuckled, then her gaze slid away from him.

"Tell me what you're thinking, Kip."

"I don't know if I can." Eyes still averted, she took a deep breath. "I never . . . That is, in all the time Marsh and I were together, there was never . . . It just never happened to me like that."

Delight rioted through him. Planting a smacking kiss on her mouth, he shouted with laughter. "That's wonderful. You make me very happy."

"Don't get too carried away. I'm not sure about any of the feelings I've had, Bear. Stop grinning."

"I can't. You've given me the best news I've ever had in my life. Don't expect scowls."

"Bear! Be realistic. This could be a fantasy."

"So what? We're both in it. That counts with me." He nuzzled her neck. "I love you."

"Oh, damn, I love you." Throwing her arms around him, she pulled him closer.

"Will you share this room with me?" he asked.

"While we live together?"

"And after."

"That doesn't make sense."

"We'll make everything sensible."

"We weren't going to rush the future." She wanted him to carry her forward, past her indecision, past her uncertainties, to where there was just the two of them. She needed him so much.

"I can't shut down my imagination," he said. "I picture you as my wife so easily."

"Really? What do you envision?"

"Let's see. Well, us together here, of course. But also having a place in the country where we'd go to be alone and unwind."

"Yes, that would be great." She smiled up at him when he chuckled. "I'm just buying into the momentary vision, not the whole ball of wax."

"I'll take what I can get."

"Tell me more."

"Well, I thought we'd have horses in the country and—"

"Dogs and cats. I like your pets. Maybe we could breed Clancy.'"

"Sorry. She's been altered."

"Oh."

"So has the dog."

"Well, we'll just get some more."

"We can do that."

"And children," she said shyly. "Are they in your mental video?"

Bear thought his heart would burst. "Children? Oh, yes, I think so." He kissed her. "If you want them."

She nodded. "I'd like more than one. I was an only child, and it was lonely at times."

"That can be arranged." He kissed her deeply, and thoughts of the animal farm and the kindergarten faded.

The storm of passion took them again, and they climbed the mountain of sensual delights, loving every sweet touch. Familiarity brought its own eroticism, yet it was all new and bright. Love insinuated itself, nothing could hold it back. Joy was a river that tossed them, took them, drowned them in the cascade.

Groggy and happy, they fell asleep, arms around each other.

May had ushered in a wet spring. But the happy look on people's faces couldn't be denied as geraniums sprouted in planters, sweet-faced petunias waved in the breezes. Even the grayness of rain-drenched days couldn't hide the wonders of the season.

Kip walked down Park Avenue, smiling as she gazed at the buds starting to blossom on the trees. Birds whirled above her, singing and dancing. Being with Bear the last two weeks had changed her perspective on everything. The world had taken on a sheen, and if there were still some shadowy corners, they were hardly important at all. Bear took away the bogeymen in her life.

When the fire marshal had told them that the fire in her apartment had been the work of an arsonist, Bear had steadied her. The extensive damage to her uncle's journals and diaries had been heartrending, but Bear had promised they would get experts to reclaim as much as possible. He had taken much of her fear away.

Even the phone call from the hoarse-voiced man, telling her to get out of town, had not been so fearsome because Bear had been beside her. And it had been he who'd informed the police.

Joy was an everyday occurrence. She could have broken into song, warbling with the sparrows and robins.

Making the early appointment the day before with a Park Avenue retailer had been inspired. She'd met Mr. Gormez for an eight o'clock breakfast at her showroom, closed the deal for the fabrics, and now she could indulge herself in the sweet, fresh day as she walked to the office. Ahhh, spring! Soon to be summer!

The light changed and Kip stepped off the curb.

It all happened in an instant. She looked up, saw the car speeding her way, and tried to regain the curb. Then she felt two strong hands lift her backward, and the car sped past.

Kip reeled. If it hadn't been for the hands supporting her, she would have fallen.

"Lady, you okay?"

"My God, did you see that?"

Concerned voices raised all around her, but Kip didn't answer anyone. Instead she stared at her benefactor. "Thank you."

"It's all right, miss. My name's Shim Locke. I—"

"I know who you are. You work for Mr. Kenmore."

"Yes, ma'am. We've been watching you just like he wanted us to."

"I never noticed you."

"That was the idea. Shall I walk with you a ways?" Studying her for a moment, he half smiled. "You're okay, aren't you?"

"Thanks to you, I am."

Looking in both directions, Shim Locke led her across the avenue. "Going to work?"

"Yes. Thank you for what you did. I certainly appreciate it." She shot the slightly built, dark-skinned man an interested glance.

"I'm American and Japanese. My mother was born in Kyoto."

"I didn't mean to stare." She paused when they reached the sidewalk. "You don't think that was an accident, do you?" The smiling face didn't alter much, but there was a masklike appearance to it now.

"No, ma'am, I don't. Black-tinted windows are almost obsolete on cars now, but not on that car. Also, he'd been on the other side for a time with his hazard lights on, seemingly unable to start his car. Then when you began to cross, he shot across the intersection."

"You're very observant." Kip tried to smile, but her knees were shaking. "And do you think that this is somehow tied to the apartment fire and the accident with the car in Detroit?"

Shim Locke kept walking, his lazy gaze seeming to see everything. "It could be, yes." He gave her a sharp look. "I'll have to tell Bear about this."

"I understand." She bit her lip. "I won't let him wrap me in cotton batting."

Shim Locke chuckled. "He'll try. Dolph said he's . . ."

Kip laughed when the man faltered and looked flustered. "I can imagine what he said. Let's hurry. I think I'm late."

When they reached her building, Kip turned to offer her hand to her protector. "Thank you again for what you did."

"Will you be staying in for the rest of the day?"

"Yes."

"Well, then I'll see you this evening . . . or one of my people will."

Kip walked into the building, then recalled she had a late-morning appointment with Marsh. She should tell Shim Locke that. Whirling around, she retraced her steps to the street to see if she could catch him, but the detective was gone. No matter, she told herself. Doubtless there was someone else around. As long as someone was watching her, they would follow her to her destination.

The morning flew by. It seemed as though she'd just donned her dress shoes before she was changing into her walking shoes again. No way would she take a taxi on a spring day. Besides, it was only a few blocks to Marsh's place.

"Myrtle, I'm going to be at Finewood's. I should be back by lunchtime."

"You should, indeed, if you're meeting Mr. Kenmore." Myrtle smiled.

Kip fought the blush. How stupid! she thought. As though it was some big deal that she was living with Bear. But it was. "I'll be back in plenty of time," she said crisply.

Walking down the stairs because it was faster than waiting for the elevator, she pondered Bear and her life with him. Everything was delightful! Without him she'd just exist.

She pushed open the door to the street and inhaled the dampish air. The sky had cleared somewhat, and there were even patches of blue.

She slung her briefcase filled with samples and her capacious leather purse over her shoulder. Marsh had evinced interest in some of her fabrics. With a little luck she could pique his curiosity about the new ones they were fashioning. It had crossed her mind more than once that their company should branch out into interior decorating. There was enough talent at Morningstar to handle the artistic end, and there were certainly demands from clients that they provide such a service. Just imagining the challenge of expanding the company was enough to put a spring in her step. Sure, she'd have to put in long hours initially, but there could be countless benefits, not the least of them being the chance to stretch artistically. And the added revenues, if everything worked out, would be most welcome.

Inhaling deeply, she crossed Fifth Avenue, taking a cross street to Madison Avenue. This time when she crossed, she looked both ways and scrutinized the vehicles. No sense taking chances. Once burned twice shy and all that.

It took under ten minutes to reach her destination. Once more she was struck by the newness of Finewood's, the added opulence. She couldn't make up her mind whether she liked it or was repelled by it. It certainly was richly appointed. That had to be a copy of a Renoir. Marsh could never have afforded the real thing. Yet it looked genuine.

Kip smiled at the receptionist and gave her name, and was directed through a labyrinth of corridors. Finewood's had owned the building for years, but they'd always rented a good share of it in order to cover operating expenses. Obviously they'd expanded, and she wondered if they were now using the whole building. And she wondered why Marsh hadn't told her. She shook her head. How badly Marsh suffered in comparison to Bear. No one could come close to Bear.

How could she ever have thought she loved Marsh? He was handsome and charming, but now when she looked at him, she felt nothing more than a nebulous loss of friendship, and not even a painful loss at that. After all, they hadn't been angry when they'd parted. In fact, Kip felt sure that Marsh had been as relieved as she at the divorce, no matter what he said now.

She finally found her way to the room indicated by the receptionist, which seemed to be above the showroom. Stopping a person who was carrying a clipboard, she said, "Hello, I'm Kip Noble. I've come to—"

The woman smiled and nodded, pointing to a door on the other side of the hall. "Of course. Mr. Finewood said you should go right in, Miss Noble."

"Thank you."

The door opened before she reached it, and Marsh stood there smiling. "Hi, come in. We'll talk, then we'll lunch."

"Now, Marsh, I told you I had a lunch appointment."

He shrugged, his smile wry. "Can't blame a guy for trying."

"Let me show you our work." In minutes, she had spread the samples on the table in his office and was describing their qualities and textures.

"These are beautiful," he said, fingering one. "But I expected to like them. We've done business with Morningstar for years."

Kip looked up sharply. "That's right. I'd forgotten that."

"Sure, that's why I bid for it at the same time your uncle did." He paused. "I still regret that I lost to him."

• • •

Bear was surprised when he called Kip, and Myrtle told him she'd gone to Finewood's. She hadn't mentioned it when she'd left early that morning. He felt a shard of discontent, of gnawing wariness. Was Kip attracted to her ex-husband even if she didn't think so? They'd shared a life, they had a history.

"But she said she'd back in time for your lunch date, Mr. Kenmore."

"What? Oh. Fine, Myrtle. Thank you. If you see her first, tell her I'll pick her up at twelve-thirty at the office."

"Yes, sir, I will."

Bear cradled the phone and stared into space. His life had done a complete U-turn when Kip had entered it. For years his focus had been on driving, then on the management of the family business. With his small circle of friends, and the many women he'd been involved with, his life had satisfied him.

Now it was different. There were depths he had to plumb, heights to scale. The world had taken on a luster that he hadn't even known was missing. She'd brought sparkle and laughter, a love-passion that seemed to have no end. And she'd done it all by simply rushing at him before he could get into her car.

"Damn!" Bear jumped to his feet, the quick motion lifting a corner of his desk blotter and scattering pencils and pen across it. He walked to the floor-to-ceiling window and looked out, drumming his fingers on the glass, not seeing the panoply of buildings, the peeping sun casting spears of light on the concrete and glass. He saw a woman, slender, curving, eyes alight with laughter, slumbrous with passion. He hit the glass a resounding smack.

"Hey, take it easy, will you. You could cut yourself if you put your fist through there."

Bear turned slowly. "Piers. Dolph. How are you? Was I expecting you?"

Dolph glanced at Piers before his narrowed gaze settled on Bear. "We've come at a bad time?"

Bear shook his head, shrugging roughly. "No. I'm just having a strange morning."

"Worried about something?" Piers sat in the chair in front of the desk, his gaze skating over the messy surface.

"I don't know. I'm being an ass, I suppose, but Kip's over at her ex-husband's, and it bothers me."

Dolph smiled gently. "That's because you love her."

"I know that," Bear said tautly. "I want to marry her . . . but she's not sure."

"Didn't you say that she had a poor experience the first time?" Piers asked.

"Yes. And I understand her reluctance. It's just that I know we can be happy together."

"Then if you know that, give it time. I had to give Damiene space."

Bear smiled. "I remember, and you chomped at the bit."

"He climbed the walls," Dolph said.

Piers grinned. "Right, but now we're together." His smile faded. "I can't stay. She could go any day now."

"Hold it." Dolph shook his head. "She practically pushed you out the door, Piers. You've been driving her crazy, dogging her footsteps every minute."

"I know, I know. I can't help it. I'm nervous. I wish I could go through it for her."

Neither of his friends laughed. They knew he was serious.

Piers shook his head. "But we didn't come here to discuss my dilemma, and since I won't leave Damiene for long stretches, I want to get on this."

Bear nodded. "Go ahead."

"Shim Locke called us because he hadn't been able to get in touch with you." Dolph watched Bear go through his messages, lifting one from the small stack. "He didn't think Kip would tell you that a car almost hit her on Park Avenue this morning."

"What!" Bear's fists clenched, his shoulders hunching as if he expected to be attacked. "Tell me."

In short, terse sentences Dolph sketched what the detective had told them. "So he said it could have been an accident, but it was pretty pat."

"I'm getting her." Bear stalked to the door, pulled it open, and left.

"He's upset," Dolph said mildly. "Guess we'd better do something."

"You do it. I have to get back to my wife."

Dolph groaned. "She'll kill me. I promised I'd keep you out for an hour."

"You failed." Piers strode from the room.

By the time Bear had fought his way through the Manhattan traffic, he wished he'd taken a taxi instead of his car.

Finally parking the Ferrari in a tow-away zone, he walked toward the entrance of Finewood's rug company. The door was opening as he approached. He stopped in his tracks when Kip walked out arm in arm with Marsh. They were gazing at each other, laughing.

Frozen, he let the rivers of people eddy around him. Images of the accident that had trapped him in the car was a fading memory in his mind, but not even then had he felt the pain that sliced him now. His breathing was constricted, his stomach knotted, his skin pearled with cold sweat. He would have turned away if he could have moved.

Kip looked up and saw him. Releasing Marsh's arm, she ran to Bear and kissed his cheek. "Am I late? I'm sorry. Did Myrtle tell you where I was?"

Bear's glance fixed on Marsh, then moved down to her. "Piers and Dolph came to the office. They told me what happened this morning."

She clapped a hand to her mouth. "I forgot to call you. Things got hectic and—"

"You forgot something as important as your life? As a car almost hitting you?" Anger mixed with fear was a snake writhing through him.

Marsh wove through a crowd of pedestrians and joined them. "Did I hear right? Were you almost hit by a car, Kip?"

"Yes, but a man saved me." She kept her gaze on Bear. She hadn't known him long, but she knew him well enough to realize he was in a fury. "Bear?"

"I think we should go now. Our reservation is for twelve-forty-five. Finewood, see you again." Taking her arm, he led her to the car, just as a traffic cop was writing out a ticket.

Seven

Bear twirled the glass in his hand. When was the last time he'd had a vodka martini with his lunch? Not since he'd taken over the company. He stared broodingly at the drink. It didn't even taste good.

"That's your second," Kip told him primly.

"You're not my mother," he snapped.

"No, but I am riding with you. Shall we order?"

He quaffed the drink and signaled for the waiter. "Why not?"

"Going to drink your lunch?"

"And if I am?"

"Then I'm taking a cab. I don't ride with drinkers."

They ordered, with Bear asking for another vodka martini.

When their steaming shrimp creole was placed in front of them, they glanced at each other, then looked away.

Bear polished off his martini. "I'll bet you'd like a white wine with this."

She put her hand on top of his. "Eat your creole."

He turned his hand over so they were palm to palm. "I don't suppose you'd like to forgive a jealous jackass who was scared to death."

"When he's sober I will."

Relief coursed through him. "I'll let you drive."

"You bet you will. You should go home and get some rest. Aren't we supposed to go to your parents' this evening?" She pulled her hand back and tasted her food, welcoming the warmth, the spice, the succulent shrimp.

Bear blinked at her, helping himself to some creole before answering. "Forgot that. Damn. I'd rather we had a quiet evening at home. I don't want to go." He struggled not to slur his words. It had been a long time since he'd had so many drinks. He'd all but given up drinking when he was racing, after a friend had been killed in a drunk-driving accident.

"I wasn't the one," Kip said, "who told them we'd be glad to visit with them. You were."

"That was a mistake. Mother will probably play her opera records, and I'll have to listen to that screeching tonight." He closed his eyes. "She loves Puccini."

"First, Puccini isn't screeching. Second, any noise at all will bother you this evening." Kip beamed at him. "You'll have a big head."

"Getting unholy glee from another's pain doesn't say much for your character. You're a sadist."

She cupped her hands under her chin. "I think I must be. I'm certainly enjoying this. Now, perhaps you'll tell me why you were doing your Attila the Hun imitation in front of Finewood's."

"Afraid of getting a parking ticket?"

"You got one. Isn't there a better explanation?"

"Yes, but I'd just as soon not go into it."

"Indulge me."

"You are a sadist." He cleared his throat. "Jealousy is an infantile, foolish reaction to anything."

"Right. Get on with it."

"I am, I am. Give me time." He drank lemon-laced water thirstily. "It made me mad when you walked out of the building holding Finewood's arm," he said in a rush. "And I was pretty jumpy to start with, after hearing what Piers and Dolph had to tell me."

"For corn's sake, we didn't have a big blowup divorce. Our marriage was a mess, but we parted quietly and without fuss, like friends. And you knew one of Shim Locke's people would be watching me. So there was no need for a fuss."

"Friends don't part," Bear mumbled.

"Don't split hairs. You were boorish."

"And I apologized."

"So you did."

"Am I forgiven?"

"As much as I'd like to string this out and turn the screw, I guess I'll have to drop it and forgive you." She grinned when he made a face at her.

"You're so generous," he told her silkily. He wished they were home, in bed, so that he could love her senseless.

"And you're still miffed a bit."

"Miffed? You misread my message, love. I was wishing we were home, in bed, with—"

"Stop that." She tried to glare at him, but the image of the two of them on the bed rose in front of her mind.

"Your face is red."

"It's been like that since I met you."

He pushed aside his empty plate. The food had made him feel better. "Why don't we go home for an hour or so, and I'll let you pull out all the stops?"

"I think you changed the subject. Weren't we talking

about the opera?" Her heart was thudding so hard in her breast, she had the feeling she was choking. Bear Kenmore made her body tingle from backbone to fingertips.

"Your husky voice excites me, Kip. And when your eyes darken that way—"

"Would you like dessert, sir?"

Bear looked up at the waiter as though the man had appeared from Mars.

Laughter escaped Kip. "Perhaps we could have coffee," she said, "decaf for me, regular for Mr. Kenmore, and a cheese-and-fruit board sounds good. Doesn't it, Bear?"

"What? Cheese? Yes, yes, that's fine. Stop laughing."

"I can't help it. Have you ever been as frustrated as you've been today?"

"Probably, but it never annoyed me as much." He sat back in his chair, smiling reluctantly. "You've certainly enjoyed yourself."

"Yes. I have the feeling that this is an historic event. Bear Kenmore put in his place! I could sell tickets."

"Very funny. Let's go home. I want to chase you around the house." She was exquisite in her Chanel suit. Taking it off her would be one of the greatest pleasures he could imagine.

"Can't do it. You might catch me."

"That's the idea."

They stared at each other for long moments.

Kip looked away first. "I should get back to work." She didn't want to. She wanted to go home with him. Would she ever be able to handle the power he exuded?

"So should I," Bear said stiffly. It irked him that she could turn off their intimate conversation so easily.

"We can't go too fast, Bear," she said quietly, staring down at her hands, clasped in her lap. They'd already plummeted into a relationship. Nothing could have been faster. Even to her ears her explanation sounded lame.

"We haven't been. I just dislike it when you turn aside our intimacy." He needed to kiss her, hold her. When they were together, naked body to naked body, there were no disagreements.

"I told you from the beginning that I didn't want—"

"Marriage. I know. But we're living together, and it's working. You can't deny that."

"I don't deny it."

"Then don't turn it aside as though it didn't mean something. It does." He stood and helped her rise.

"I wasn't doing that. You make me sound like a capricious child."

"Well put."

She glared at him. "Just because I don't want to catapult into an emotional maelstrom doesn't make me a baby."

"Doesn't it? Shall we go?" Lord! he thought. Were they beginning to sound like an acerbic couple, married a hundred years?

Stiff and walking apart, they barely acknowledged the farewells of the maitre d'.

"No need to drive me," Kip said. "I can catch a cab."

"It's no trouble," Bear said. What he would like to do was start the conversation over, settle things between them, knock down the barrier they'd erected just while eating lunch at Chez Orlean.

In the car they said nothing.

Kip felt as though she'd explode. When Bear stopped in front of her building, she had the car door open and was out before he could come around and assist her. "I'll see you this evening," she said. "Don't pick me up after work. I'll walk."

"As you wish." And he'd make sure she had a guard.

He drove away, his fingers drumming steadily on the wheel, frustration and chagrin chewing at him. He hadn't even asked her if her meeting with Finewood had gone well, if she'd accomplished all she'd set out to do. Nothing was said about her fear when the car almost missed her. She would've been frightened. And he hadn't even asked her about it! Instead of arguing with her, he should have been comforting her.

Kip watched the car disappear in the traffic and felt an ineffable sadness. Why couldn't she say what she felt with Bear? He made her feel secure that she could be open with him. What held her back? She'd gone over many times the deeply bred reticence to commit herself. It couldn't all be her marriage that caused it. Could it?

She walked inside the building, heading for the elevators. What had there been between Marsh and her that had eroded their marriage anyway? Had she ever pinpointed that? Had she tried? She could recall a feeling of relief when she'd discovered for sure that there were other women in his life. It had given her concrete reasons to broach divorce. Even with that, Marsh had been shocked that she wouldn't even consider reconciliation or counseling.

She still had no sure answers why her marriage had been shaky from the beginning. There had been more than just the infidelity that had forced dissolution of the union. That had just been the catalyst. But she had never delved too deeply into what might have been the real reasons. She'd just been glad when it was over.

Uncle Phineas had seemed to dislike her marriage intensely. Had she listened too much to her uncle and not enough to her husband? Would there have been reasons to stay with Marsh if she'd listened to a counselor, if she'd deigned to see one? Had she let her uncle interfere in her marriage? Had she been infantile about an adult problem? Was that the reason she was afraid to trust her future with Bear?

"Are you getting off on this floor? You pressed for it."

Kip looked blankly at the man who'd spoken, then nodded and left the elevator.

Rushing into her office, she brushed past Myrtle's desk.

"Miss Noble. Did Mr. Kenmore find you?"

"Yes, he did. Any messages?"

"Yes, Mr. Finewood called. He'll call back."

"Fine." She smiled for the first time since entering the office. "It looks like Finewood's will be sending us a big order."

"Good. Mr. Finewood is nice. But so is Mr. Kenmore."

"Yes, both of them are fine."

"Miss Noble, are you all right? You look a little pale."

"Fine." Kip walked into her office and closed the door behind her, leaning against it. Even Myrtle had begun to compare them, just as Kip had done countless times. There was no comparison. Marsh just didn't measure up to Bear. Besides, she loved Bear.

There was a knock on the door. Kip stiffened. "Yes?"

"Miss Noble, I thought I heard you groan. Are you all right?"

"Yes, I am, Myrtle. Just looking at the piles of work I have."

Myrtle's chuckle vibrated through the door. "I suppose we should be glad we have the orders."

"Right." Kip opened her eyes and stared at her desk. How was she supposed to concentrate when Bear was foremost in her mind all the time?

The phone rang as she crossed the office. "Kirsten Noble speaking."

"Kip, I can't keep saying I'm sorry, but I am." Bear

rushed his words, wishing he was with her. His head was pounding, and he was mad at himself for pouring down the vodka. Damn fool!

"Bear. Oh, Bear, so am I." Tears of relief clogged her throat. "I don't want us to fight." She gulped back a sob. "I think we could make each other ill."

Her husky voice ran over his skin. "Are you crying?" Her vulnerability coupled with her unusual strength made her sexier than anyone else on the planet. Sweet toughness! He loved that.

"I'm being foolish," she said. It had torn her in half to be angry with him. Were lovers like that? What other new plateaus would Bear introduce to her?

"Really? Then I won't tell you I feel like crying."

She laughed. "That I'd like to see."

"Should I come over there and demonstrate?" Her laughter buoyed him; her tears shredded him.

"No. We both have heavy schedules. I'll accept that you're a sentimental guy."

"And I also eat quiche and have offered to diaper my godchild when she or he arrives. I'm not sure what category that puts me in, lady."

"The right one for me."

"I'll have to fight to keep my head from swelling." Had they just committed to each other? Or was he reaching?

"Stalwart person." Her spirits had risen sharply simply by talking with him.

"I'll admit to being a little shaky about the diapering."

"But undaunted."

"True blue."

She hesitated. "Bear, Marsh and I talked about business, about my uncle's car, about the Morningstar building." She inhaled shakily. "It looks like he's going to purchase some fabrics from us, a sizable order."

Bear sighed. "'Honey, I was stupid, and I don't want you to think you have to explain anything to me."

"I want to explain, I want us to keep talking. We do well when we do that." She caressed the mouthpiece of the phone with one finger, as though she could touch him. "You know what I mean."

"Yes. I wish I was there with you, and if I didn't have a meeting in fifteen minutes I would be."

"I feel the same." Had he gasped, or had the sound come from her? No matter. She was reeling with the sensual grip Bear had on her, and the want and need she felt for him. "I look forward to seeing you this evening."

"No more than I, sweet one. Wear something casual when we go to my parents, preferably a burlap bag. I'll be staring at you all night, and I don't want to look like a lovesick puppy."

She laughed, delighted with the easy footing they'd regained. "You won't."

"I could over you, but since I don't really give a damn what anyone else thinks of us, it's no big deal." Her mirth eradicated all the hard spots in his mind and heart, the nasty rawness that had overcome him when he'd seen her with Marsh.

"Won't your parents object if you look too vacuous?" she asked.

"They'll know I'm in love."

There was a cessation of sound, even of breathing. The air vibrated over the connection.

"Those are nice words, Bear." Nice! They were everything to her, all she'd ever want to hear.

"I want you to like them." He felt as though he'd handed himself to her, given her rights over him that no one had ever had.

"I do."

"Sounds like a vow."

"Does it?" She couldn't control the shivery sensation that passed over her.

"I'll pick you up at six, Kip."

"Bear—" She heard the click as he disconnected. She put her head down on the desk, pillowing it on her arms. "Bear," she whispered, quite sure she could disappear in the aura he created.

Bear cradled the phone. He wanted a commitment from her. He wanted her love, her body and soul. It was only fair. She had his. Yet he wanted it all freely given, not pulled from her. If backing away and giving her space was the love gesture he had to make, he'd make it. But it was damned painful.

Kip had not only gotten under his skin, she was throughout his system.

The phone rang.

"Kenmore. What? Well, get on it. Now." Work gripped him like a vise. The overseas subsidiary in Germany had had a fire. Then it was the meeting, hours of phone calls, damage reports, head count.

At the end of the day, Bear was relieved that none of the Kenmore Motors employees in West Germany had been hurt, though the fire had destroyed some valuable equipment. Finally he was able to leave the office, and he hurried so that he wouldn't be too late picking up Kip.

Gridlock snarled traffic at almost every block. Bear cursed in a low, steady stream, vowing to let Phelps pick them up from then on. But he knew he wouldn't do that because he relished the closeness he and Kip shared in the car.

As he pulled up to the curb in a tow-away zone, he

watched her leave the building. As always, her lissome form drew his eyes, her easy, strong stride accentuating her beauty. Getting out of the car, he walked toward her. "Hello, darling. I missed you."

"Me, too," she said. "And I think you're about to get another ticket." The blue fire of his eyes warmed her. And as always, that wonderful sense of safety filled her. She loved that about him. He was the sexiest man she'd ever known, but it was his caring she loved most.

Bear turned to see a traffic cop approaching. "Whoops. In the car." He closed her door, then sprinted around to the driver's seat. Firing the powerful engine, he engaged first gear and pulled away from the curb into the throng of cars.

"Shall I wave?" Kip asked, laughing.

"Please don't. I want to spend the evening with you, not in jail." He reached out a hand to her after he shifted again.

She put her hand in his, feeling his warmth at once. It was late May, but the evening air had a bite to it. Bear's touch warmed her inside and out. "Tell me about your parents."

Bear looked startled for a moment. "I'm so used to them, I don't know if I could describe them. They've always been there for my sisters and me. As I said, they live in Puerto Rico most of the time. But they do have the big place on Long Island that they visit on occasions." He paused. "They're important to me."

"I understand that. I had Uncle Phineas, and most times that was enough for me, but after he died, I had to face up to the fact that I had no more family. Many times I'd wished for a sibling."

"Now you have me."

She chuckled, coming out of her gray moment. "Now what would the racing groupies say about that?"

"I don't know and I don't care. Besides, I don't race anymore." It was his turn to laugh when she grimaced at him.

"Rat."

"I wasn't a groupie guy, Kip." He shot her a quick look. "Honest."

Such a rush of pleasure went through her, she felt giddy. "You don't have to explain to me."

"I want to explain. There were women in my life, some of them important, but you're the one I want to clean the slate for, to make things smooth for, to live with, to share my home."

"Wow. Big important stuff."

"You still want to stop by the house and change?"

She nodded. Actually she'd prefer him to drive across country with her, holding her hand.

Bear loved to bandy words with her, but her silences were just as exciting. She made him come alive. And he'd found out more about himself since meeting her. He'd always loved children; now he wanted hers. He'd figured he might marry one day; now there could be no one but Kip. She was everything he'd ever dreamed of, and more, in a life partner.

When the car phone buzzed, he was reluctant to release her. "Hello?" He looked at Kip. "Phelps said Finewood called about an order."

She nodded. "I should call him about that."

Bear spoke into the phone. "We'll be dropping by the place for a minute before we go out to the Island."

"It would be easier on you," Kip said when they reached his house, "if you let Phelps drive. Then you could ignore the traffic."

Bear shrugged. "True, but I like us to be alone."

"Me too."

He kissed her cheek.

Phelps opened the door for them. "I left the message on the desk in the library, Kip."

"Thank you. Excuse me."

Bear stood with Phelps and watched her walk down the hall to the library. "She's beautiful, Phelps."

"I know. You'd better get ready. Your folks are expecting you. Your sister Janine and her newest flame will be there. And Nedda and Clark. So will your aunt Venezia."

"What?" Bear snapped out of his daydream. "I'm not taking her then. I don't want her barraged by that gaggle."

"Nice way to talk of the family," Phelps sniffed, walking away from him.

"I don't care, I mean it."

Kip dressed in record time, even though she'd been puzzling over Marsh's call. Why would they need to have lunch together to talk more about the order? That seemed overdoing it.

She and Bear had not discussed her sharing his room, though she shared his bed every night. She sighed as she looked around the Green Room. Maybe it was just as well. It gave them both a measure of autonomy.

Uneasily Kip studied her reflection before she left her bedroom, noting her pale lemon-colored satin suit with the cinched-in jacket and small peplum, the very straight skirt that hit midcalf in several long, stark side pleats. With it she wore an even paler yellow chiffon blouse and black patent low-heeled shoes with a patent leather clutch purse.

She left the room and was startled when she saw

Bear come out of his room at the same time. "I thought you would have been ready ages ago."

He grimaced. "I'm not that thrilled about going. According to Phelps they'll have a circus there."

She blinked. "Oh."

"Don't worry," Bear said grimly. "If they start to rattle their cages, we'll leave."

"I'm sure your mother would be delighted at your description of the family."

"You'll agree with me once you meet them." Bear shook his head, his gaze going over her. "You're so beautiful. Not many women would dare to wear that shade of yellow. It would make most look sallow, but on you, it's wonderful."

"When did you get to be an expert on women's clothes?" Kip could have bitten her tongue. That slow smile of his made her raise her chin defensively.

"I'm not an expert on women's clothes," he said. "But I do want to be an expert on you." Heat suffused him. "I'm not trying to put you off, darling. I want to pull you closer."

She sighed. "I'm resisting. I admit it. It's because I'm so drawn to you, Bear, not because I want to be away from you."

He took her in his arms and kissed her gently. "Let's go."

They walked out of the house to the car, holding hands.

Kip leaned her head back against the headrest and watched his strong hands on the steering wheel. "I love your hands," she said softly.

Bear steadied the car when it jerked under his grip. He didn't look at her, and it was a few moments before he spoke. "Kip, do you like living together as much as I do?"

"I like it very much," she whispered

"I want us always to be together. Sleep together, eat together, share our lives, our work, our moments apart, and our moments together. I want that."

"Does this mean you want us to share the same closet?"

He jerked his head around her way. "You bet. How about you?"

"Bear, watch it, you'll be crossing the highway dividing line." She put her hand out, touching the wheel.

He covered her hand with his, slowing the car. "Tonight?"

"Tonight what?"

"Tonight I hang my sports coat with your skirts." He grinned. "That's sexy."

"Bear! You're crazy."

"I'm serious. Stop laughing."

"Can't. I'm happy. Will you think about tonight?"

"I already have. We'll do the switch when we get home. What a momentous occasion."

"And I have to be driving. Damn!"

"And not that well for a world-class performer." Trills of laughter escaped her when he glowered at her. "Struck a nerve, did I?"

"Yes." But Bear didn't care. She was happy. And she'd made him happy.

Kip couldn't keep her eyes off his strong hands as they controlled the powerful machine. She could recall how they felt on her body. Heat suffused her, and she looked away.

The traffic was bad, but Bear knew a couple of short-cuts, and they were able to make good time.

When he turned up a drive and she saw the pile of stone and mortar hugging the knoll, she gasped. "It's beautiful."

"It's a barn of a place, but there was lots to do here as a kid."

"I'll bet." She caught a glimpse of people milling about near a large structure behind the house. "What's going on?"

"They're probably looking at the new filly. Father bought a thoroughbred in Ireland. It was probably shipped here, then it'll be taken to Kentucky in a few days."

"You have a place in Kentucky?"

He nodded. "A horse farm. My mother's from Kentucky, and she's always had horses."

"I never learned to ride."

"I'll teach you."

"On a low horse I hope."

"How about a burro, so your feet drag on the ground?"

"Perfect." The trepidation she'd been feeling about meeting Bear's family melted away. Nothing could halt the well-being that coursed through her. She and Bear would be a team. And what a team.

"I like the smile on your face," he said. "I hope I'm in the daydream."

"You are." She reached over and stroked a finger across his mouth. "What's your smile signify, Kenmore?"

"I was thinking of the time we met."

She closed her eyes. "I'm not proud of knocking us both to the ground, but I was angry."

"You're a tiger, sweetheart." He chuckled, turning his head to kiss the finger on his face. "Loving the tiger in you won't put me out of your dreams, will it?"

"You're still in there."

"Good, because you're in all mine."

"Why, Mr. Kenmore, suh, you'll turn my head." She fluttered her eyelashes at him.

"If you bat those eyes at me, I might let go of this wheel and we'll land in the paddock along with the newest purchase." He rounded the final curve in the drive, then sped to a stop under the portico. "Didn't mean to jar you against your seat belt, Kip. I was distracted. You drive me wild."

"No excuses." She let her gaze rove over the large house. "The stonework looks purple in the sunset." His words made her light-headed. Bear said the darndest things. If only she didn't react to him so quickly.

He grinned and cupped her neck. "If that's heat I see on your face, I empathize."

"Don't jump to any conclusions," she said tartly, turning back to the house. "Tell me about the masonry." Tell her anything to get herself back on keel.

"All right, I'll change the subject, Kirsten Patricia. But we'll get back to talking about us. The granite was brought from a quarry in Italy by my great-grandfather."

"You have been here a long time."

"Before that the family was with Jesse James. That's how they made the money to build this place."

Laughter curled out of her. "I'm going to tell your mother."

Bear shook his head. "She's not the one to tell. Mother's very proud of our checkered past. And it's no end of frustration to my father that she's writing a book about the Kenmore who ended up on the gallows. Mother says it'll be a saga. Father's planning on suing her."

Kip gasped. "That's a lie. How can you talk about your family that way?"

Someone opened the passenger door, reached down, and took Kip's hand, helping her from the car. "Is Bear dragging out the skeletons again? He's as bad as Mother. Hello, I'm his sister Nedda, the only sane one. The others are at the barn and dying to meet you."

Bear looked over the top of the car and groaned.

"Mother said you were here. I'd been hoping you were out of the country."

"I'm back." Nedda grinned at him. "I wanted to meet your girlfriend."

"Cute, Nedda. Where's your husband?"

"Forget it, Bear. Clark won't help you. He's on my side. You'll like Janine's newest. He's not at all impressed with us, and he's crazy about Janny." Nedda grinned. "Mother and Dad like him. Poor guy, he's done for."

Bear shook his head. "No doubt."

"Come and meet him." Her smile included Kip.

Kip watched the siblings, catching the affection under the barbed banter. Nedda looked remarkably like Bear, the same attractively strong-boned face that was softened by a warm smile. When Nedda looked at her again, she stuck out her hand. "I'm Kip Noble."

"I know." Nedda grinned and pulled Kip's arm through her own. "Let's go. It'll drive him wild."

"Nedda! Come back here."

Nedda hurried a laughing Kip along toward the barn.

Bear glared at his sister when he caught up with them.

Nedda kept up a running commentary about the family, the estate, and her husband. "And you and I have to talk at length, Kip. There's definitely a service you can render to the women of the world."

"See," Bear whispered. "I told you it would be a circus." He put his arm around her possessively.

Nedda grinned. "I can't believe what I'm seeing." She sighed dramatically. "It finally happened to you. There's still justice in the world." Before Bear could answer, she turned and waved to the people near the stables. "Here she is and all in one piece." Nedda's clarion call carried to the group.

"Damn them," Bear muttered.

Kip laughed, then turned toward the older woman walking toward them, her well-worn jodhpurs enhancing her tall, straight figure. Kip reacted to the warm smile by holding out her hand.

"My dear, welcome to our home. I'm Candida Kenmore. Most people call me Dee." She smiled at her son. "Beryl, you can release her. We're not going to eat her."

"I'll see to that," Bear said.

"All the Kenmores are like that," Dee said conversationally. "I must tell you about Abner Kenmore. He was hanged, you see. Unrepentant to the last." Her smile widened when Kip laughed. "Oh, I think I'm going to like you."

"Mother," Bear said warningly. He put out a hand to reclaim Kip's, but a man who was an older version of himself passed him and took her hand instead. "Father." Bear didn't mask his irritation.

"Hello, young lady. It's nice to meet you. I'm Thaddeus B. Kenmore. I knew your uncle. He was an honorable man." He clasped her hand with both of his.

Kip nodded. Nothing he could have said would have pleased her more. "Thank you."

Bear saw how moved she was. He reached around his father and pulled her close to him. "Darling." He kissed her hair.

"Wow." The whisper was loud in the sudden stillness.

"See, Janine, I told you," Nedda said, almost crowing.

"Isn't it great to see him flattened?" Janine said with obvious relish. Janine, like Bear and their mother, had thick dark hair and beautiful blue eyes. Tall and slender, she was lovely.

"Now, girls, be good," Dee said mildly. She winked at Kip. "Oh, dear, here comes Aunt Venezia."

"Mother," Bear said through his teeth.

"It couldn't be helped, my boy," his father said softly. "She owns one-half of the filly."

Kip watched the woman, who could have been anywhere between sixty and ninety, approach. Her carriage was erect, her mien stern, her body angular and in good condition. The well-worn jeans didn't look incongruous. Though her hands and face were wrinkled, her eyes were glinting and perceptive.

Kip unconsciously straightened, tucking her tummy, and lifting her head.

"So you're the one who's knocked Mr. Wonderful on his posterior, are you? I'm Venezia Beryl, Dee's aunt, and Beryl there is wishing me back in Kentucky this very moment."

Kip took the proffered hand, inclining her head politely as she'd been taught in Miss Winter's Private Academy for Women just outside Zurich, Switzerland. She fought to contain the amusement that rose in her. "How do you do?"

"Choking with laughter, that's what she's doing, Dee. Maybe she'll help you with the book on the nefarious Kenmores." Venezia Beryl chuckled.

"Over my dead body," Thaddeus muttered, and frowned when his wife pinched his arm.

"Isn't this going to be fun?" Janine said, rubbing her hands together.

"Hell," Bear said softly, keeping his arm around Kip.

Janine gestured to a brown-haired man and introduced him as Charles Rogers. "Isn't he cute, Kip?"

"Very." Kip answered Janine's impish smile. She also noticed that Charles didn't seem to mind anything that Janine did.

The next hour was a whirlwind as Kip met the new filly, the stable hands, the household staff.

At dinner Bear winced more than once, but the irrepressible Kenmores couldn't be contained.

Kip loved it, finding her footing and joining in the rousing after-dinner debate over politics. Only she, Aunt Venezia, and Dee were liberals. They attacked the conservative Kenmores lustily.

"Red in tooth and claw, isn't she, son?" Thaddeus whispered to Bear. "Reminds me of your mother. Never could tame her," he added with satisfaction.

"If anyone is tamed in our relationship, it will be me, Father, and not Kip," Bear murmured.

Thaddeus's shout of laughter turned heads toward him and Bear, but neither man explained.

Eight

In the days following their sojourn to Long Island, Kip heard from both of Bear's sisters and his mother, lunching with the latter and enjoying it very much.

"Kip, my dear," Dee told her, "we welcome you to the family with great joy."

"But . . . but, Mrs. Kenmore, I mean Dee, I'm not in—"

"Never quibble about small things, my dear. Aunt Venezia has said you've knocked Beryl on his, ah . . . backside, and we agree."

Kip didn't quibble. She liked being friends with Bear's family.

Dee leaned across the table. "And you've unfrozen him, given him back the warmth he needed in his life. For that I'm grateful."

When Kip wasn't working, she was with Bear. She delighted in the moments and hours with him, feeling as though she'd entered an entirely new phase of her life. It was a freewheeling, spinning, controlled chaos that melded laughter, hard work, and love. She had resisted, not wanting to get caught up in his thrall, but it hadn't worked. She was wrapped in the golden threads of desire, curiosity, fun, joy, and a seemingly everlasting anticipation of being with him. Never had she felt so liberated . . . or so tied. She was bound but unfettered, flying but anchored. It was wonderful, yet she still felt discomfort. Was she giving away too much of herself? She'd done that in her marriage, and the repair time had been long and painful.

When Kip studied Bear, though, she couldn't fault him. He held nothing back, yet he demanded little. His feelings were there for all to see. So, could it be wrong if hers showed too?

It was dealing with her own feelings that had her stymied. The rivers and mountains of sensations and reactions were novel to her. Marsh had never made her feel anything like what she felt when Bear looked at her. The fear of giving herself over to anyone again had been with her for a long time. Ridding herself of it was not going to be easy, and though with Bear she'd been more open about herself than at any other time in her life, the fear of being too open was strong.

Kip shook her head, caught in the aura of memories. It had been only two months since she'd driven from Detroit to New York with Bear, but it seemed like years. She'd entered a whole new life, and the one before grew ever dimmer. It was as though she'd been sleeping before and was now truly awake and living.

When the phone rang at her elbow, she reached for it eagerly, sure it was Bear. "Yes?"

"Kip, how are you? It's Marsh. I wondered if you're free for lunch today. You put off our last engagement, and I was hoping we could meet today."

She grimaced. She'd put off their lunch because she really didn't want to see him. He was a jarring memory.

She wanted nothing to disturb the wonderful present. "I've so much work today, Marsh. I was just going to have something at my desk."

"Don't be silly. I have a reservation at Geronkin's. You know you love their food."

"That's a chain, Marsh. I liked the food when we were in Detroit, but tastes change and—"

"Fine, I'll reserve a table at a little French place I know. Do you know where Chez Artistes is located? I can swing by and pick you up if you like."

Kip sighed. She had the feeling it would be easier to get rid of Marsh if she lunched with him. "It's not that far from here. Twelve-thirty?"

"See you then." Marsh rang off as though he feared she would change her mind.

Kip put her head in her hands and cursed quietly. She'd counted on her lunch hour to munch on her natural peanut butter sandwich and map out a schedule of deliveries that she could submit to her clients and suppliers . . . and maybe have a few moments to think about Bear. It was the time of day when she could indulge her daydreams of him, and that had become so important.

The time until lunch sped. At twelve-fifteen Kip reluctantly gathered her things, planning on stopping at the bank on her way back to the office. "Myrtle, I'll be gone until after two, I think. I'm going to Chez Artistes for lunch, then I'll stop at the bank."

Myrtle consulted her calendar. "You don't have a lunch date." She looked up at Kip. "And you brought a sandwich today."

"You eat it," Kip said absently. A glance at her watch told her she was behind time.

Running, she caught the elevator just before the door closed. She could have taken the stairs, but a sudden lethargy had overwhelmed her. Damn Marsh. There were a thousand things she'd rather do than have lunch with him.

"And you say she just left for lunch, Myrtle?" Disappointment flooded through Bear. "All right, I'll call her when she returns. Is she lunching with a client?" Damn! He'd wanted to tell her that Piers had called earlier and said that Damiene had gone into labor.

"I think so," Myrtle said, "even though the date must have been made today. I don't have it on my calendar."

"Thanks. I'll call later." Bear cradled the phone, then glared at the picnic basket on his desk that held a bottle of chilled sparkling water, Gruyère and Camembert cheese, English water wafers, a loaf of French bread, wineglasses, cloth napkins, and two red roses. It was ridiculous to feel down, he told himself. He was going to see her for dinner. The gloom didn't leave him.

Reaching over, he grasped the napkin-wrapped bottle and opened it. He never looked up when the door opened. "Go away."

"How did he know it was his dear friend, I wonder?" Dolph strolled to the desk and took another bottle from the basket.

"Because you and Piers," Bear said, "are the only ones who enter my office without knocking." He glared at Dolph and gulped the spring water.

"I can tell you're glad I'm here." Dolph slumped down in a chair after pouring a glass of the water. "Could I have some lime, mine host?"

"Help yourself."

"You sound as though your best friend has deserted you." Dolph pawed through the basket, taking out the cheeses and a small, sharp knife. "Umm, grapes too. Properly washed, I hope."

"Go away," Bear said sourly.

"Could this good friend be a woman? Kirsten Noble by name?" Dolph popped a grape into his mouth.

"Yes. I was sure she had a free lunch day. When I called, she'd just left, to meet a client, I suppose." He smiled tightly when Dolph laughed. "Yeah. I know. It's stupid. Tell me about it. It doesn't change how I feel."

"I know that. I remember how Piers was with Damiene." He glanced at his watch. "I can't stay long. I have to get back to the hospital."

Bear looked sheepish. "I'm a fool. I should've asked right away. How's she doing?"

Dolph dropped a pile of cigars on the desk. "I know you don't smoke, but I thought you'd like a little remembrance of your goddaughter's birth. Eliza Jane by name."

"A girl? Damn, that's wonderful. That's what I'd like."

Dolph's arched eyebrow pointed higher. "Pardon me? Making an announcement?"

"Don't be cute. How are Damiene and the baby?"

Dolph chuckled. "She was fine when I saw her, right after she had Eliza Jane." He gestured with his thumb toward the picture of Piers that sat on the table to one side of Bear's desk. "He was taking oxygen when I went into the room, and clutching her hand as though it were a lifeline."

"Was it rough for her?" Bear asked with concern.

"It was a long ten hours." Dolph smiled. "Piers told me he wanted it to be him going through the labor."

Bear nodded. "See how you feel when it happens to you."

Dolph looked at his shoes. "It won't."

Bear cursed his insensitivity. "Sorry." There was no

helping Dolph with his dark side. Both he and Piers had tried at other times. Would they ever know the full story? "So help yourself to the picnic and tell me about my godchild."

Dolph ate a square of cheese, looking at him narrow-eyed. "Announcing Eliza's new name wasn't my only reason for being here. Something's come up, old chum."

Bear sat forward, his mouth tightening. "Is it about Kip?"

"Maybe." Dolph wiped his hand on a linen napkin, his gaze never leaving his friend. "One of my body-guards mentioned to Shim Locke that there have been rumors floating around over the last few years of suspicious shipments delivered to Kip's company, Morningstar Fabrics. This information came through a rather intricate pipeline from the Treasury Department and Interpol. It looks good, but it could be bogus." Dolph folded his hands in his lap and looked calmly at his friend as Bear surged to his feet.

"What the hell does that mean? You can speak plainer than that."

"Sit down, Bear."

He did so, reluctantly. "Go on."

"Her company has been investigated by the feds more than once because of suspected drug smuggling, though they've found nothing. It seems that the imported fabric business could have been a front for a more lucrative business." Dolph paused. "Admittedly no evidence of any value has ever been found."

Bear sat back. "But you don't think it's all smoke, do you?" His hands curled into fists on the chair arms. "Phineas Noble had a spotless reputation, and Kip isn't capable of doing anything dishonest. I'll do what I have to, to protect her and her name."

Dolph nodded. "I have to get back to the hospital and

hold Piers's hand." He stood up. "I sure as hell wouldn't have bothered coming to you with this if I thought Kip was guilty. You'd just pick her up and cart her out of the country."

"Yes, I would."

"I'm being straight, Bear. You know that."

"Right." Bear squeezed his forehead with one taut hand. It was as though his world were fragmenting. He could almost smell danger. Fear swept through him at the uncertainty of it. Who? What threatened Kip?

"Piers knows about this," Dolph said, "but we haven't come to any rock-hard conclusions, Bear. It just seems peculiar that her shipments have been zeroed in on more than once. It could very well be coincidence."

"But that's not your real feeling about it, is it, Dolph?"

Kip watched Marsh, trying to concentrate on what he was saying and trying not to yawn. She'd rather be back in her office working than lunching with her ex-husband. What was Bear doing? she wondered. Was he eating lunch?

She saw an inquiring look on Marsh's face and knew she should have responded to something. "I'm sorry. What did you say?" She almost smiled as his mouth tightened with irritation. Marsh had a giant ego. He thought all women hung on his every word. "Too many work details pressing in on me," she murmured.

"I thought that might be the trouble. That's why I'm prepared to make you an even better offer than I did the last time, Kip." Marsh sat back, looking satisfied. "I can take that white elephant off your hands."

"Better offer? You mean for Morningstar Fabrics?" She stirred her coffee for a long time before she looked at him. "I thought I told you I wasn't interested in selling, Marsh."

"You did." He shrugged. "But you've admitted you're tired, that you've had to work very hard—"

"Everyone works hard, Marsh," she said tiredly. "That's the name of the game when you own a business. But I like what I do, just as Uncle Phineas did."

"And you're as stubborn as he was." Marsh smiled tightly.

"You call it stubborn, I say it's determination." She looked at her watch. "I should get going. I have a mountain of work."

Marsh leaned across the table and grasped her hand. "Kip, we've always been friends."

"You could call it that."

He frowned. "I've always cared for you. I thought you felt the same."

"Marsh, get to the point."

"I want to be the first one you turn to when you do sell—"

She pulled back her hand, annoyed. "Don't you listen? I'm not going to sell. It's my legacy from Uncle Phineas, and I'm going to make it work."

"And do you think Kenmore would want his wife—or live-in—to work in what he could describe as an inferior business?"

Kip felt the blood rise in her face as anger, discomfort, and a new razor awareness filled her. "Look, Marsh, don't make assumptions—"

"Am I wrong in saying that you live with him?"

"What I do is none of your business. I don't inquire into your personal life, and you don't have the right to query my actions."

Marsh shrugged. "So be it. I still think you might be in the market in a few months. Will you call me first?"

Grasping her purse, Kip rose to her feet. "It won't happen. But if by any chance it does, I'll call you. Good-bye, Marsh." She left the table almost at a run, not looking left or right. If she didn't get into the fresh air, gulp some oxygen, and try to process the unpalatable truth just flung at her, she might burst.

Bear would be ashamed of her business? Admittedly it was small in comparison to a conglomerate like Kenmore's, but it was hers, and it was in the black.

A sense of bleakness pressed her down, so that she could barely lift her feet.

What did Bear think of Morningstar? He'd never said, not really. She'd no more give up her business than she'd ask him to give up his. But how did he feel? Damn Marsh. He was always able to pick through the top layers and find the irritating nucleus. All of her efforts didn't blank her mind to what he'd intimated about Bear. Did he think her business small-time and expendable compared to his?

By the time she reached her office, she was out of breath and out of sorts.

Myrtle looked up, reaching for a sheaf of notes.

"I'll take the messages later," Kip said shortly, sailing into her office. "Hold the calls."

Twenty minutes later when her phone rang, signaling a call was being put through, Kip glared at the instrument, then answered it. "Kirsten Noble."

"Hi," Bear said. "Myrtle told me you didn't want to take any calls, but I wanted to tell you that I'm a godfather. Damiene had a baby girl."

"She did? How wonderful. Tell me about it."

Bear told her how Dolph had described Piers's anxiety, his mood lightening when she laughed. "And I wanted you to know that I missed having lunch with you."

Kip's heart lurched. "You did?"

"I did. I arranged a picnic, then called and found you'd gone out to a business lunch. I was pretty blue."

"I was pretty miserable too. I had lunch with Marsh—"

"I didn't know. I wouldn't have interfered," he said tightly.

As though a flashbulb had gone off in her head, she understood his feelings. "It was a last-minute change of plans, and believe me, I wish I hadn't gone. It was the same old pressing me to give up the business. Around and around we went."

"Tell him flat out that you're not selling, that it's yours, you like the work, and you're good at it."

Kip took a deep, shuddering breath. "Do you mean that?"

"Of course I mean it. I'd give you a job in our corporation if you weren't so caught up in your own work. You're good at what you do, you're enthusiastic, and you love it. Why would you think I wouldn't know that?"

She paused.

"Was Marsh putting bugs in your ear?"

"Yes, and I must say it shook me, because I've always considered you such a feminist. I didn't think you'd feel threatened by my working, having my own career."

"Damn him, did he say that?"

"I know it's foolish of me to get upset by—"

"I'm coming over. I'll be there in fifteen minutes."

"But—but you can't. Your work . . . my work . . ."

"The hell with it."

Kip stared at the dead receiver, then replaced it slowly, shaking her head. Bear Kenmore was a hurricane.

Less than ten minutes later her office door burst open.

"Hi. I'm here."

She grinned. "I think I know that."

"Do you?"

"Yes."

He came around her desk and took hold of her upper arms, lifting her to her feet. "How are you?"

"I've been better." He kissed her gently. "I love you and I like you."

She cupped his face in her hands. "That's nice."

"Nice? Hell, it's more than that." He hadn't known how much he'd missed her until he'd heard the uncertainty in her voice when they'd talked on the phone. That had scared the hell out of him, made him madder than he'd been in a long time. "I trust you, Kip. I want you as a friend. And I want you in my life forever."

"Commitment," she said weakly.

"Yes. How do you feel?" He didn't breathe as he waited for her answer. His entire being hinged on it. "Tell me."

She stroked his cheek. "I love you and I like you." Bear lifted her into the air and whirled her around until she squealed.

"I love you, Kip."

She smiled down at him, not trying to hide any of her feelings. He grinned and snuggled his face between her breasts.

"Put me down," she said, laughing.

He let her slide down his body. "Will you marry me?"

She hesitated. "Could we live together for a little while longer?"

Bear nodded, not entirely able to mask his disappointment. "You know it's all right. We'll do it your way." He grinned again. "But I'll still keep asking."

"Please do." She reached up a finger and scored it down his cheek. "Shall we eat at home and cook something special ourselves?"

"Let's. How about stopping at the fish market and

getting some of those soft shell crabs from Florida that you like so much?"

She nodded, her hand cupping his jaw. "And fruit, and bread."

"And cheese. We'll have our French picnic, a little more elaborate, but wonderful."

"Yes." She kissed him, her mouth lingering on his.

"Kip! Don't, sweetheart. I won't be able to leave. And Myrtle will have something to be shocked about."

"Right," she said breathlessly, quite sure that the heat she saw in his eyes was mirrored in her own. Her arms still tight around his neck, she added, "See you later."

"I'll pick you up." He bent to kiss her again.

The kiss went on and on, their bodies pressed tightly to each other, spinning away into the beautiful kaleidoscopic vortex that was their own.

"Ah, pardon me," Myrtle said cautiously, not quite able to hide her smile. "The Winter's representative is on the phone and wants an answer right away."

Kip lifted her head, blinking. "Oh? To what?"

Bear looked around at Myrtle, his smile rueful. "Some day I'll strangle you, Myrtle," he said gently.

"I know," she said, trying not to laugh.

Kip wriggled free of Bear's hold. "All right, I'll take it. 'Bye. See you later."

He kissed her nose. "Count on it." He swept by Myrtle, making a face at her.

Kip looked at her secretary, her hand hovering over the receiver. 'You're fired."

Myrtle grinned. "Again?"

Kip worked hard all afternoon, the many snags almost welcomed. Every time she had a free moment, she wanted to call Bear. The pull of work didn't quite bury those feelings.

What had happened between them had cemented more firmly in her mind that he was all of the future for her. She desired him and loved him.

Throwing down her pen, she buried her face in her hands. Marriage! Could she face it again? Wasn't living with Bear enough?

Her intercom buzzed, and Myrtle told her Mr. Dworkin was on the line. She picked up the phone immediately.

"Hello, Mr. Dworkin. How are things at the factory?"

Harold Dworkin was in charge of the Morningstar factory down on Third Avenue, and she talked to him nearly every day. She also visited the factory at least once a week.

"Yes, I know about the shipment," she went on. "Is there something wrong? You're not sure. All right." She looked at her watch. "Maybe I could stop by on my way home. No need for you to stay. Just leave me a note, and I'll check the paperwork. If I don't make it this evening, I'll go in early before opening. What time do they remove the dogs? All right, either way I'll stop by. And thanks for calling."

She replaced the receiver and cupped her chin in her hands. She'd always enjoyed going to the factory and particularly liked to walk through the warehouse, with its sky-high piles of wrapped fabric. It was part of the beauty of the business she loved.

Mr. Dworkin had sounded anxious about seeing her, so perhaps she'd make the effort to go down there after work. Then she remembered her picnic dinner with Bear. Maybe they could swing down there on their way to the fish market.

•　•　•

Bear couldn't keep his mind on his work. Finally, he jammed a few files into his briefcase and called Morningstar. "Myrtle? Tell Kip I'll be there in five minutes."

The drive to Kip's office seemed interminable, even though the traffic was not as bad as it had been other times he'd picked her up. He needed to be with her, to hold her, to have her brush her lips against his neck. His whole body shivered with delight at the thought.

Leaving the car in a yellow zone, he ran into the building. He didn't wait for the elevator, but took the stairs two at a time to her floor.

Sprinting down the hall, he stormed into the outer office. "Hi, Myrtle. Is she ready?"

"She better be. Boy, are you impatient." Myrtle pulled her purse from the drawer. "I guess we're closing up early today."

"Good idea," Bear said fervently, then grinned when Myrtle laughed out loud. "Have a good evening, Myrtle."

"Oh, I will." Myrtle was still chuckling as she left.

Bear opened Kip's door. "You have to lock up. Myrtle's gone."

Kip smiled at him. "I'd better hurry. You're probably in a 'no parking' spot."

"Yeah. I'll help you put things away. Tell me what to do." He tidied her desk while she put the final touches on a staff memo, and within minutes they were leaving the office.

Bear noticed her quick frown as she locked the door. "What is it?"

She looked at him, seeing the fire behind the concern. She wanted that fire, needed it. "Nothing. I'll take care of it in the morning. I hope you won't mind if I get up before dawn tomorrow."

He smiled slowly. "Who knows? You might still be awake."

She pretended to be cross with him, even as she blushed pink with delight. "Lecher."

"Yes, about you I am." He kissed her. "Maybe tomorrow we can take a long lunch and visit Damiene and the baby." He kissed her deeply. "Babies are nice. I'd like a girl first."

"Bear," she said, breathlessly, laughing. "You are taking quantum leaps."

"Not really. I believe in planning. And planning a family takes care and concern."

"Are we doing that?" she asked as they stepped into the elevator.

"Oh, yes. We're planning many things."

Miraculously, there was no ticket on the Ferrari, nor any policeman in sight. Bear laughed as he pulled out into traffic.

"I feel lucky today," he said. "You make me feel that way, Kirsten Patricia Noble."

"Do I? Well, what do you want to do on your lucky day?"

"Shower with you, make love, maybe make a meal, and—"

"No maybe about it. I'm hungry." She laughed excitedly, her body warm and wanting.

"No shower? No lovemaking?"

"All those, but food too. Don't forget the fish market. And we'll have more fruit and cheese. I assume you and Dolph finished the other."

"Yes. It was good." Bear accelerated, swinging easily around another vehicle and speeding ahead.

"You're a good driver," Kip murmured, putting her head on his arm. "I like a great many things you do."

"Do you love any part of that?"

She glanced up at him, smiling. "There are a great many things about you I love."

He turned and smiled at her. Horns blew around them. "You do pick your times, Kirsten Patricia."

"I thought you'd want me to tell the truth."

"Truth like that I want to hear anytime." Bear had never felt such heat suffuse him. "I love you, Kip."

Such a simple declaration, so unadorned, she mused. He'd made it before. Why did it seem so new, so wonderful? Why was the blood cascading through her veins, her body lighting up like a torch? "For a real cool guy, laid back and all that, you can say some hot things. Whatever happened to Black Frost?"

"You melted him, darling."

The trips to the fish market and vegetable stand were made in record time.

Nine

They were home. They put the food in the refrigerator, then, arms around each other, strolled into the front foyer, dropping their briefcases along the way.

Halfway up the stairs, they kicked off their shoes, taking no notice when they tumbled back down.

"I'm glad Phelps won't be back until tomorrow," Bear murmured.

"We should prepare the food first," Kip said, turning her back when they entered the bedroom so that Bear could undo the one button at the back of her blouse.

"Umm, we should." He helped her slip out of her skirt.

"We can shower later," she said, and took his hand to lead him to the hot tub. "It's amazing."

"What?"

"I do love looking at your—your body." Kip stared up at him. "That's a new sensation."

Her simple revelation made him want to shout with victory. He'd always been well aware of his worth, in all areas of life. If that was conceited, then he was. But never had he felt so powerful, so wonderful, as he did at that moment. He kissed the palm of her hand. "You've given me a great compliment, my lady, and I won't forget it."

"Am I your lady?" she whispered, pressing her lips into his thick black hair.

"Oh, I think so." He moved back and put his hands on her waist. Gently he lifted her down into the water, then pressed the switch on the wall to start the action.

Stepping down beside her, he prevented her from sitting. When she looked up at him inquiringly, he smiled. "I like looking at you too, beautiful one." He laid his hand between her breasts. "Your blush goes down even farther."

She lifted her chin. "Know it all."

"I could never know enough about you." Leaning down, he took one breast into his mouth and sucked gently. When he heard her shuddering sigh, his libido galloped into action. His hands tightened, and he pulled her closer. Kneeling in front of her, he ran his mouth over her skin, nuzzling her soft breasts.

Kip threaded her hands through his hair as she bent over him, her breath coming in short gasps. "Bear." It was only a wisp of sound.

"Yes, my sweet, I'm loving you."

"I know."

They sank down into the warm swirling water, Kip cradled in his arms. The heat of their bodies was greater than that of the water, and Bear took her suddenly, lovingly. She cried out and clung to him, arching up to meet him. Water cascaded over the sides onto the surround, until their wild motions ended with their shuddering releases.

Bear sighed, his face against her neck. "I never wanted it to be that fast, sweetheart."

"Me either," Kip said with surprise. "But I was ready."

Her shining eyes had his heart thumping again. "I hope you won't get up and run screaming into the night when I tell you I still want you."

"Since I feel the same, I'll try to control myself." He lifted her out and began drying her. "Give me a towel. I want to dry you."

"Good." He obligingly turned around and let her dry him, wincing when her fingernails scored lightly down his back.

"Hurt?" she asked.

"You know what it's doing, Kirsten Patricia Noble."

"Yes, I do." She chuckled. "You certainly like my full name. You use it all the time."

"I'm just looking forward to the time when it can be changed to Kirsten Patricia Noble Kenmore. Nice, huh?"

Kip stopped drying. When he turned, she looked at him gravely. "I thought we decided marriage was on hold for a time, Bear."

"No. You decided, and I went along with it, but that doesn't mean I won't push for a wedding."

She gazed down at her feet, then up at him again. "I won't try marriage until everything in the relationship is ironed out, talked over, and decided on, Bear. I went that route once and ended up wondering what I did know about my husband. I don't want that again."

"Fine. We'll live together, and you keep probing. I'll keep answering until it's all out where you can see it."

She licked dry lips. "Can't you see it's good for you too?"

"You're good•for me," he murmured, scooping her into his arms and racing from the bathroom.

"Why are you running?"

"Don't want you to catch cold." Bear hid his down-hearted feeling. He wanted to tell her how much he needed her, how good it would be with them married, how simple all problems would seem if they were a twosome. But he said nothing. They would be a twosome, just not a married one. If that was the way it had to be, he'd be content with it.

Kip pressed her face into his neck, holding tight to him as he followed her down to the bed. "Am I wrong in thinking we'll be making love again?" she asked. She'd sensed his hurt and hated that.

"Not at all," he murmured against her breast, then lifted his head. "Unless you'd rather not."

"I'd rather." She pulled his mouth to hers and kissed him greedily, her tongue dueling with his.

The satin sheets slid sensually against her body as Bear moved closer to her on the bed. She arched up to him.

"Kip, you're a sensual voluptuary. Is that redundant?" His words were slightly slurred.

She saw the slumbrous heat in his eyes as his gaze went over her. She pressed against him again, the rough-sweet friction exciting her.

When she felt his muscles tighten and swell, she was sure her body would burst into flame.

With Marsh it had been so different. Even when she'd been sure she loved him, she'd only striven to please, not sought or expected pleasure. Now she wanted the heat and wonder that only Bear could give her. She wanted his heart, his passion, his love, and she wanted it desperately. As much as she delighted in giving him sensual excitement, she wanted it back in full measure. She was greedy for his passion.

She ran her hands over his body. "I trust you," she said softly, wonderingly.

"Thank you. And I trust you."

"We have dark corners," she said through lips gone dry.

He raised himself over her. "If this isn't what you want tonight, we can stop."

"It's what I want," she said, her hands threading through his hair, "but we have to be straight with each other."

He kissed the corner of her mouth. "It's what I want too, and I know that you hold back some of yourself, darling. I accept that, but I also know that the time is coming when we'll be fused together, mind, heart, and soul, and it's soon."

"Oh, Bear." She gulped a sob and pressed her mouth to his. "I love you." Her hands closed on his waist, shock waves running through her at the touch of him.

"Sweetheart, I love you, and I know you. You're tough, eager, determined, gracious, spunky as hell, and innovative."

"Keep going," she said in a teary voice, pressing her body to his, loving it when he gasped.

"If we're talking, you'd better not do that," he said hoarsely.

Kip felt his excitement flow into her, and anticipation thudded through her bloodstream. She wanted Bear more than anything, more than peace of mind, more than joy, more than life.

Feathering her hands over his bare chest, gently tugging at the black hair set her on fire. Her elemental need for him transcended all the common sense and right choices for which she prided herself.

Bear gazed down at her, her lustrous eyes limpid with passion, her skin glowing with an inner heat, and he knew he had in his arms all that he'd ever wanted or needed. The rest of his life would fall in line. The ice that had packed his soul and mind cracked and melted because one sweet woman held him, flooded him with life. There was no holding back.

For the first time he needed no barriers. Even if Kip cut him to ribbons with her love, he'd never hide from her. He'd welcome every slash. He was hers, and that made him happy.

"What are you thinking?" She kissed the corner of his mouth.

"About you, about us, about how committed I am to you."

"Oh." Her throat tightened, air struggling from her lungs. No one had given so much of himself to her, not ever.

Touching his nipples was not just erotic curiosity but a necessity. Acting on impulse, she slid down and closer, pressing her mouth there, sucking gently. Her desire spun out of control.

Bear groaned, his hands tightening on her, his mouth seeking hers.

The kiss was a covenant.

Kip exploded from within, her soul linking to his for all time.

Bear reeled from her power. She'd delved deep inside him and melted all of the black ice.

Their passion rose swiftly, and they joined together. Body to body they clung to each other as they sought and found the ultimate joy, the giving and taking of elemental love, the unselfish possession of woman by man and of man by woman, the golden treasure which so few find.

They came together in crashing cacophony of wonder, of love newborn and mature, of passion freshly spawned yet older than time. Excited cries mixed with groans of fulfillment.

They held each other for long moments, bodies slick

with satisfaction, neither wanting to break the bonds of sensual love.

Bear pushed her hair back from her forehead. "Darling, you're beautiful. Was it good for you?"

"Outstanding." She smiled languidly when he laughed. "It was. I can't make a fist. See." She held up a limp hand, then let it fall to the bed. "My goodness, this is really an aerobic exercise." Her eyes fluttered shut.

"The best." He yawned hugely and cuddled her close to him. "I love you."

"Me too," she managed faintly. Then she was asleep.

When she woke the next morning, Kip was still in Bear's arms. She turned to look at him, reveling in the freedom she had to study the man she loved. He was beautiful! And she wanted nothing more than to waken him and make him love her again. Unfortunately, duty called.

She planted a soft kiss on his chest, then gently freed herself. When she got out of bed, she couldn't resist watching him for a minute more, then she sprinted for the shower.

Dressing hurriedly, she studied her reflection in the mirror. Yes, the coral-and-brown tweed suit was flattering. She snatched up her brown leather handbag, scratched a quick note to Bear, and raced down the stairs.

Phelps met her in the morning room off the kitchen. "Early bird," he said, setting down fresh squeezed grapefruit juice and vitamins. "Oat bran cereal and muffins this morning, with eggs, ham, homemade bagels, and—"

"Juice, cereal, one muffin, no coffee, thank you." Kip had learned not to turn down all the food, or every bit of it would be set in front of her. Phelps believed in hearty breakfasts. Besides, she was hungry. She and Bear had been too absorbed with each other the night before to bother with food.

"Bear won't think that's enough," Phelps said.

"Then don't tell him."

"I don't think it is either." He frowned at her and left the room, returning almost at once with her breakfast.

"I would háve preferred a bowl rather than a bird-bath," she muttered after he'd gone back to the kitchen. She ate all she could, finished the juice, took two bites of the muffin, then escaped to brush her teeth.

Hurrying, she made it down the stairs again and out the door before Phelps could tell her he would chauffeur her. It was barely light out, and she thanked her stars she was able to hail a cab quickly.

She got to the factory at a little after six. The dogs were supposed to be taken away at six, and either the night watchman or Dworkin should be there. If for some reason neither were, she had her own keys. And Dworkin had said he would leave her a note.

As the cab pulled away, she studied the factory-warehouse. The place looked abandoned without the hustle and bustle of the people who worked there, but she felt lucky to own such a fine piece of real estate in Manhattan. If her uncle hadn't had the forethought to renovate the building instead of selling it, as many had pressed him to do, she wouldn't have the convenient and very suitable place to store the fabrics that were imported from all over the world.

She stepped up onto the platform and pressed the bell. When a minute passed and there was no response, she tried again, then she took out her keys and unlocked the door.

Once inside, she stared around the immense interior, noting with pleasure the careful stacking of material.

Satisfied that all seemed to be in order, she made her way to Dworkin's glass-enclosed office off the main warehouse area.

She had to use her key again to unlock the door, and she spied at once an envelope with her name on it on the desk.

Sitting down behind the desk, she pulled a sheaf of papers from the envelope and began reading. Having expected information about a shipping problem, she was shocked to read that Dworkin suspected the warehouse was being used to stash stolen goods.

How long she sat there reading in the ponderous silence she didn't know. But a prickling at the back of her neck told her she wasn't alone.

She looked up and blinked in surprise. Marsh was standing outside the office. "What are you doing here?" she asked as he opened the door. "Did Dworkin let you in?"

Marsh stared at her for a long moment. "No, I have my own key. I've had it since shortly after our marriage, when I asked your uncle's permission to have some of our rugs delivered here."

Kip was taken aback. "I didn't know that."

"There was no need for you to know. It only happened a couple of times." He shook his head. "Why did you have to interfere with the running of the warehouse? It would have been so much easier." He smiled ruefully at her deepening surprise. "After a time your uncle forbade me to use this place, but I kept my key. What are you reading?"

Strange sensations tingled through Kip. Marsh seemed . . . weird. She was uncomfortable with him. Had he told her why he was there? "What am I reading?" she repeated, confused for a moment. "Oh, this is pretty upsetting. Dworkin accuses people of using the warehouse for keeping stolen goods and asks my permission to—" She stopped when Marsh suddenly slapped his hand down on the papers. "Hey, what are you doing? Stop that. And come to think of it, get out of here." She glared at him and held out her hand. "I'd like that key you have to my warehouse."

"No, I can't do that. He said he didn't write anything incriminating, but I didn't believe him. He's so like your uncle. Neither understands big business."

Processing the unpalatable information was speedy enough, but Kip didn't want to accept it. "Are you saying that Dworkin told you about this?"

"Oh, I'm sure you'll read my name in that report somewhere."

Marsh's smile made her skin crawl, but she forced herself to stay relaxed. "Is all of this mixed up with your constant pressure to buy Morningstar from Uncle Phineas and now from me?"

"Yes. It looked for a while as though Granger was going to be able to handle it, but you didn't scare, did you?"

"Granger? He works for you?" At his nod her hand curled into a fist. It was his friendly smile and conversational tone that made her shudder. She forced herself not to look away from him. "The accident with the car? The fire?"

"All Granger, and very clumsy. That's why I decided to take charge myself." His smile widened. "I was always able to handle you, Kip."

"Was this warehouse the reason you married me?" She didn't care a fig if it was, but she needed to keep him talking so that she could think.

He leaned closer, his smile twisted. "Yes, you could say that, but I do admit that marrying you was easy.

You weren't great in bed, but your frozen-goddess mien attracted me mightily."

It flashed through Kip's mind that Bear wouldn't describe her as frozen anything. Bear! He was the warmth in her life. She could get out of this, reason with Marsh. "Marsh, give it up. Whatever you've done it's not worth risking everything. You're not in too much trouble now. If you back off, I can forget the whole thing."

"Forget? You? You're like a dog with a bone, my sweet. You wouldn't rest until you found out what happened to your uncle and old Dworkin."

A cold wind iced her heart. "My uncle?" Her voice was little more than a croak. "What do you mean?" When Marsh cocked his head playfully, dread had her shivering. "Tell me."

"The old boy had a heart attack all right, but I helped him along, Kip, my sweet. Knockout drops in his wine, then a big shot of digitalis. He'd confronted me with my . . . er, little sideline, and I had to protect myself."

"Sideline?"

"Ah, still intellectually virginal, are we? Well, Kip, old girl, the real world dictates that we survive, any way we can. Importing exotic products such as—"

"Drugs." Slowly she stood up. "You killed my uncle because of drugs. Damn you, damn you." She didn't know she was going to heft the marble pen set until she threw it with all her might. Before it had even struck him, she was around the desk and running for the door.

Survival! Marsh was going to kill her. She had no doubt of that. After telling her all of that, he had no choice. Uncle Phineas! And Bear! She wouldn't see him again unless she outthought Marsh Finewood.

Sprinting across the cavernous building, she tried to keep the piles of fabrics between her and her chaser.

"Don't bother running, Kip. Even if you do get outside, I have a gun in my car. If I have to, I'll get that and use it on you. Why not be a good girl and come back here? I'm watching the only exit, and I promise to make it as painless as possible."

She made a sharp right turn and paused to remove her heels. Gripping her purse as her only possible weapon, she headed for the stairs that would take her up onto the high catwalk.

Bear turned over when the alarm went off. No, it was the phone. Even as his hand lifted the receiver, he thought of Kip. "Kip? Where are you?"

"This isn't Kip, old man. It's Dolph. Wake up and listen."

His friend's sharp tone cleared his mind. "Go."

"We got hold of a guy named Granger. He was spotted by one of Shim Locke's men at the airport. They pressed him pretty hard before turning him over to the police." Dolph paused. "He admitted to tampering with the car and setting the fire. He paid one of Kip's mechanics a large sum of money."

"Damn," Bear whispered.

"It seems he works for Marshall Finewood."

Bear sat bolt upright. "Her ex-husband. You think he's involved in something crooked, and in deep enough to bring the feds sniffing around her warehouse?"

"We don't have anything solid, but a picture is beginning to form. And it could make a lot of sense. Where is Kip?"

"I don't know. Maybe she's downstairs. I'm going to

find out. Cover this for me, Dolph. And I'll want more protection for her."

"It's been done," Dolph said tightly. "This morning."

Bear rang off without answering and raced downstairs to the kitchen. Only Phelps was there. "Where is she?"

Phelps shook his head. "She left in a hurry. I can see this is important, but I don't know where she is. She left you a note."

"Get it and bring it into the bedroom." Bear washed in record time, then dived into jeans and a shirt. He was tying his running shoes when Phelps entered the bedroom. "Read it."

"I have. She went to her factory. Want me to drive?"

"No. Stay with the phone. Call Gunder, Piers, and everyone else, including the police. Tell them where I've gone and that I'm damned worried. Give me the note."

Phelps handed him the keys. "Bring her back."

"I intend to."

Bear wouldn't be able to recall later how he got to his car. The first clear thought that pierced his consciousness was a horn blaring when he cut out another driver. Shaking his head to clear it of black concentration, he settled into getting to his destination speedily and without incident.

The icy reactions that had earned him the name Black Frost on the track were part of him now. Those frigid feelings had kept his driving calculated, on the ground, and in the winning column. Now they focused on Kip.

He knew where Kip's warehouse was because they'd driven by it one evening on their way home from dinner. Weaving in and out of traffic at a ridiculous speed, he sped down Second Avenue. The other drivers might have been statues for all the attention he paid them. Getting to Kip was his only criterion, his life force. If he had to drive on the sidewalk to do it, he would.

The side street that flanked the warehouse was quiet. A few trucks were parked along it, but he saw no people. There was, he noticed as he got out of his Ferrari, a Mercedes sports car, looking very out of place. Trepidation crawled over him. Who'd driven the Mercedes?

Moving as quickly and quietly as possible, he leapt onto the loading platform and tried the door. It opened without a squeak. He moved inside and closed it behind him, then stood still to orient himself. The semi-darkness was barely broken by the light of a weak bulb high on the wall.

When he heard a voice call out not far from him, he pressed himself into the shadows.

"You heard me, Kip. Come down. I know you're up there. You'll only get hurt when I come after you."

Bear thought the voice was Finewood's, but he wasn't sure. The enormous building was like an echo chamber, making it difficult to recognize a voice or to pinpoint the origin of it. If it was Finewood, where was he? Where was Kip? Upstairs? Why?

Straining his eyes, he peered upward. Had that been a movement on the catwalk? If only he could call out to Kip or see more clearly. But then the gloom was a plus for him too.

Taking a deep breath, he crept slowly around the stacks and bales of fabrics. He had to find Kip and take care of Finewood . . . in that order.

After what seemed like hours he found a set of narrow steel stairs leading up to the second level, and perhaps beyond to the shadowy catwalk.

When he took hold of the railings he paused, feeling a vibration that told him someone was above him and moving. Down or up? He wasn't sure. He had to chance it.

Taking a deep breath, he climbed to the second level. He saw no one and started up to the next. He'd almost reached the third level when he glimpsed the outline of a person in front of him. Crouching into the ladder to remain unseen, he eased upward. Then he saw Kip— and so did Finewood.

"Ah, I found you, Kip," Finewood said, stepping onto the catwalk. "You shouldn't have tried to run."

Kip rose to her feet, her hands out in front of her. "I won't go along with you, Marsh. I'll fight. Give this up, for God's sake. You can't win."

"I have so far, my dear, and profitably. That's why I can't have you interfering. You know, I plan on marrying again one day. Good for the image, but it'll be a woman much younger than you, one who will know her place."

"You talk like something out of a bad Victorian novel."

Kip looked around her. She was on the top catwalk, and it seemed like miles to the main floor. Off to her right, suspended from the ceiling, was the block-and-tackle boom used to hoist the materials to various levels of storage. She calculated the distance to it. Six feet? eight? Ten? It was hard to tell. Could she do it? Did she have an option? She knew there was a control on the end of the hook, for sending it up or down. If she could leap to that, maybe she could lower herself to another level. Maybe.

Perspiration beaded her body. It was a chance in a hundred she could do it. But it would be better than meeting Marsh head-on.

"I've always hated that tart tongue of yours, Kip. If

you'd been the right wife, none of this would've been necessary."

She moved closer to the railing, then stopped. She'd seen movement on the stairs. Who? Friend of Marsh's or hers? Either way she'd have to take some action. Unless that person could fly, he wouldn't reach the catwalk in time to help . . . if that was his intention.

Her gaze locked on Marsh. She took hold of the railing, preparing to throw herself over it. Marsh started toward her, smiling maliciously. Her heart pounding furiously, she flung one leg over—then froze. Bear! He was there below her, on the second catwalk, climbing up onto the railing.

"Bear! No!"

Bear threw himself up into the air, toward the block and tackle a few feet above him. His desperation fought against gravity, reaching for the impossible as Nature tried to pull him down to mortal level.

His fingers touched, grasped. Fear of losing Kip had him arching his body over the tackle as though it were a trapeze, rocking it, thrusting it into furious motion to carry him to Kip.

He was aware of Finewood turning his way, his mouth open. Was he yelling? Bear didn't know. A roaring filled his ears, as he focused on the fearful Kip calling out his name, her arms outstretched.

It was eons. Seconds. Then his leg curled around the railing, and he was bringing the boom to rest, hooking it over the wooden barrier.

"Look out!"

Kip's scream chilled him as he turned to meet Finewood's furious charge.

The catwalk left little room for maneuvering away from the loader's hook Finewood held over his head.

Instead of retreating, Bear rushed him, grabbing him

around the middle and lifting, trying to avoid the hook. The force of the collision sent both men against the railing, rocking the steel catwalk. The swinging motion overbalanced them, the narrow railing not enough to hold the two men as they tipped over it and seemed suspended in air.

Bear caught himself when he was half over, dangling for a second. Then Kip's hands were there, clutching him desperately.

Sobbing, she called out his name, pulling at him with all her strength. "I won't let you go. I won't, I won't."

He threw one leg around a support. Her tugging gave him just the stability he needed to hoist himself back onto the catwalk.

Finewood had no such anchor. His flailing arms and legs caught nothing. He sailed over the railing, his body arcing like a diver's, his scream echoing in the cavernous building, the loading hook still in his hand.

Bear righted himself as Kip flung herself into his arms. He held her tightly. "All right, darling. I have you, and I'll never let you go."

"Please, please promise me you won't. It was awful. He did terrible things—"

"I know. Thank God Dolph called me." He hugged her hard.

She leaned back and looked up at him, her eyes tear-drenched. "Will you marry me?"

"Yes, Kirsten Patricia Noble, I will. I love you." He saw her gaze go past him, down into the dim interior of the building. "I'll go down and check, darling."

"I'm going with you." She shivered and moved closer. "I sometimes wondered if I was frigid, because sometimes when he touched me, I was repelled."

Bear didn't pretend to misunderstand her. "That was

your subconscious telling you of danger, and that he wasn't the man for you."

"Do you believe that?" she asked as he led her to the stairs.

"Yes."

"So do I."

Bear went down a step so they were eye to eye. "Believe I love you, will you?"

"Yes, I do. Believe the same, will you?"

"Oh, yes, sweetheart. I'll never forget your proposal." He smiled and kissed her gently.

They were so engrossed with each other, they barely heard the scuffling sounds below.

A powerful beam of light picked them out on the stairs, causing Bear to curse and Kip to laugh.

Ten

Bear kept her close to him during the police questioning, answering all queries. Somehow he managed to gloss over her past personal involvement with Marsh.

She was glad to learn that although Mr. Dworkin had been badly hurt, he would live.

When they were finally able to leave the police complex, she breathed a sigh of relief, but her smile was tremulous as she looked at Piers and Dolph. "Thank you for coming when you did." She shook her head. "I wanted to see your baby, Piers."

"You will. Since you'll be marrying the godfather—"

"One of the godfathers," Dolph interjected roughly.

"Pardon me." Piers grinned at his friend, then looked back at Kip. "I will tell you that Damiene gave her wholehearted blessing on this. She wanted nothing to happen to you or her favorite race-car driver."

"Maybe her favorite man," Bear said, smiling easily.

"Not on your life."

Dolph coughed lightly behind his hand. "He lived for a short time only, Kip, long enough to tell us where the drugs were stashed in the warehouse, wrapped in rugs."

"I didn't know." She barely controlled a shiver. Marsh had been greedy . . . for nothing. "He killed my uncle." Fresh tears sprang to her eyes.

Bear tightened his hold. "Darling, I'm sorry." He looked at his friends. "Maybe we could put this off until later."

She shook her head. "No, I want to know. What happened with the rugs?"

"From what we've been able to put together," Piers said, "the rugs have been kept here since before you met Finewood. He had a deal with the previous owner. Apparently Finewood never expected the place to be put on the market as fast as it was, or that your uncle would make the buy." Piers touched her hand. "Even after your divorce, he made use of the place. Your uncle might have discovered that he was smuggling drugs and faced him with it."

Bear nodded. "Sure. He'd be in a bind. He couldn't have risked someone else finding the stash. He was caught between a rock and a hard place."

Dolph opened his mouth to speak, then looked at Bear and subsided.

Kip caught the look. "I'm sure that's why he married me, Dolph. He all but admitted it. I still feel sorry for him."

Bear kissed her.

"I don't want to seem pushy," Piers said, "but I was wondering if you're going to invite us to the wedding."

Before Kip could speak, Bear intervened. "We're getting married on the island. When we come back, we'll have a reception. You're invited to that."

Kip started at him wide-eyed.

"I think this is news to the bride," Dolph said.

"Is it unwelcome?" Bear didn't even know he was holding his breath until she shook her head, and a big sigh escaped him.

• • • •

Two days later Kip was wearing a pale coral silk gown that whipped around her ankles and gold-thonged sandals, and carrying a bouquet of frangipani.

The chapel was open to the air, and a throng of islanders watched as the lei-draped minister heard their vows.

Bear couldn't take his eyes from her when Kip said the ancient nuptial vows. His own answer was huskily spoken. "I do."

"I now pronounce you man and wife."

In the ensuing uproar of good wishes, Bear managed to pull his wife close to him and kiss her soundly. "You're mine now, Kirsten Patricia Noble Kenmore."

"And you're mine, Beryl Kenmore, darling." She turned to throw her bouquet to the throng, then she stepped from under the grass-roofed enclosure into the hot sun. " Even though this is the Caribbean, the customs seem almost Hawaiian."

"In some ways they're parallel," Bear said, grinning happily.

"You're very excited about something."

"Darling, how you talk. I'm excited about being married to you." Bear laughed, never having experienced the peace and well-being he was enjoying then.

Balmy breezes whisked around them as they held each other. The crowd had drifted away to a canopy-covered table where there was fruit punch, fruits, and cheeses.

"You have a secret," Kip said.

"Not for long." He took her hand and walked her to the table. "Let's have something, then we're out of here."

"What? No wedding cake?" She wouldn't have cared if they shared an Oreo cookie. Nothing mattered but

Bear, being safe with him, having him safe, painful uncertainties behind them.

They shared spears of pineapple and drank the tropical fruit juice. Bear watched her closely, and the moment she placed her glass on the table and turned away from the fruits and cheeses, he took her hand.

"Now what?"

"You'll see."

He led her away from the throng, who shouted their farewells. He and Kip waved back but didn't pause.

When they rounded a curve on the white sand beach, he pointed. "That's our transportation."

"An outrigger?" Kip asked, gaping at the crew of muscular islanders who waved to them. "Where are we going?"

"One more tiny secret."

"Bear!" Arms akimbo, Kip was about to give him an argument. She was bursting with curiosity.

When he caught her around the waist and lifted her high in his arms, the words were swallowed. She had all she could do to hang on when he began running toward the huge canoe.

The men were laughing as Bear placed her in the center of the craft and clambered in after her. Within minutes they were far out on the sea, the aquamarine swells rapidly carrying them away from the island.

Bear cradled her in front of him. "What do you think?"

"It's wonderful! We're flying and so quietly." She smiled up at him, loving the thickness of his black hair, the auburn highlights glinting in the bright sun.

"Look over there," he said, pointing.

"Another island?"

He nodded, tightening his hold on her.

With a whoosh of power the paddles went up, and they cruised right up onto the beach, the craft rocking fiercely for a moment.

Bear leapt out into the ankle-deep water and lifted her into his arms. "Say good-bye to your taxi drivers, love."

She waved over his shoulder.

The men laughed and waved back.

Bear let her slide down his body until her feet touched the sand, but continued to hold her as they watched the outrigger and its crew out of sight.

She turned to him, smiling. "Alone at last."

"It's taken a hell of lot to accomplish that. Come on, I want to get you out of the sun."

"How can you do that if I want to go swimming?"

He studied her secretive smile. "What do you have in mind?"

"This." She unhooked the small clasp that held the swath of silk around her. Pirouetting swiftly, she unwrapped the material from her body, then slipped the silken panties, her only undergarment, down her legs.

She was well aware that her husband hadn't taken his eyes from her. Wriggling gently to get her panties past her ankles, she stepped out of them and kicked them to one side. "Last one in gets to cook and clean up tonight." Sprinting for the water, arms wide, Kip had never felt so happy or carefree.

Bear watched her for a moment. "You beautiful little devil," he murmured, more intrigued and titillated than he'd ever thought possible. He stripped down in seconds and raced after his wife.

Kip surfaced and looked around her, knowing Bear would be close. When his head appeared in front of her, she laughed out loud and reached for him. "I love you so much."

"And I love you." At that moment he reached the pinnacle of happiness in his life. Excitement, serenity, passion, peace were an exotic tangle within him. "No one has ever given me what you have, wife. No one." He kissed her, his mouth moving urgently over hers.

"And what is that?" Kip had never felt so fulfilled, so joyous. Much of the pain of her life had been dissolved by the man who held her. The uncertainties and vague, disquieting disappointments were but a dim memory.

"Relaxation, amusement, delight," he said. "All that unnecessary stuff." He glanced toward the island, well aware of the riptide that appeared from time to time near where they were swimming. "Time to go in closer, lady." Grasping her around the middle he towed her to shallower water.

"Macho man."

He grinned, then swallowed salt water. Coughing, he stood and held her in front of him. "Brat. Making me swallow sea water."

She leaned against him as they walked to the beach.

Bear paused to scoop up their things, then led her to a stone walk shaded by royal palm trees. "Let's stay in the shade." Gazing down at her, he gulped and swallowed hard. He was like an unfledged boy with her. "Looking at you is one of my favorite things to do. You're very beautiful."

"Thank you." Kip hesitated in the shadowy coolness, facing him. "Shall I tell you what you've done for me?"

Taken aback for a moment, Bear nodded, his heart thudding heavily in anticipation.

"You've given me my very first, very dearest friend. You. Oh, I have other people I'm close to, chums and pals whose company I enjoy . . . but with you I have my primary confidant." She chuckled. "When I was a little girl, I had my huggy blanket. I wore that out. Now I have you."

"Well, you're welcome to try to wear me out," he said softly, not touching her except with his eyes.

"I intend to, even though I think you might last longer than my huggy blanket. I had to give that up when I was three."

"I will last longer than that."

"I want you to last forever." She reached out and trailed a finger down his cheek. "You have soft skin, but strong bones in your face. I like that."

"Then I like it too." His body was hardening in response to her.

She smiled and pressed close to him. "You gave me a confidence in myself that I didn't even know was lacking."

"I'm glad." He turned her and urged her on to a lovely little cottage. "Tell me more," he said as they stepped up onto the roofed lanai.

"What we have . . . well, it was different with Marsh." When his mouth tightened, she put her finger to his lips. "Our relationship is so much better. Not just our intimate life, though that's wonderful. It's everything. I could rarely get a point across to Marsh. He always seemed to override anything I said or did, any decision I made. And I was far too independent to enjoy that." She smiled sadly. "For all his modern talk, I think he had Victorian ideas about women. I can remember feeling, almost from the time of the wedding, that I'd made a mistake. When I did get around to divorcing him, it was such a relief. It was like lifting a weight from my neck." She shook her head. "I'm sorry for the pain his family must be experiencing."

Bear lifted her and carried her across the threshold, then set her down in the dim, cool foyer. "I'm glad he can't touch you anymore, Kip. I'm glad he's out of our lives." He kissed her eyes, her ears, her hair. "I don't know how long I can cuddle you like this." He was out of breath, her satiny skin making his mind explode with sensual reactions. "You're too sexy."

"That's the idea." She loved the heady feeling of power it gave her to have that effect on Bear. She rubbed her cheek against his.

"Go on with what you were telling me," he said roughly, walking her slowly through the bungalow.

"After I met you, dealing with Marsh was like handling a cream puff. I didn't let him streamroll me, or interrupt me. I did the talking. I lost the sense of confusion I'd always had with him. I stopped thinking of myself as abrasive and pushy, and realized that he was manipulative." She released a shuddering sigh. "All I felt when he died was a deep sense of pity."

"I promise you that you'll never need to face ogres of any kind again."

"Thanks." She kissed his bare chest.

"Don't do that if you want to keep talking," he told her hoarsely as they entered a spacious bedroom that overlooked the sea.

"Maybe I have something else in mind, husband." She kissed him with a wonderful urgency, and he returned it with equal fervor.

They touched each other with familiar caresses. Their desire rose at once, and they clung together, kissing again and again.

Because they needed each other. Because the bed was so close. Because they couldn't help but love. They did.

The world faded away, and only dreams of today and the future remained.

Passion and love had melted Black Frost forever.

THE EDITOR'S CORNER

Those sultry June breezes will soon start to whisper through the trees, bringing with them the wonderful scents of summer. Imagine the unmistakable aroma of fresh-cut grass and the feeling of walking barefoot across a lush green lawn. Then look on your bookstore shelves for our striking jade-green LOVESWEPTs! The beautiful covers next month will put you right in the mood to welcome the summer season—and our authors will put you in the mood for romance.

Peggy Webb weaves her sensual magic once more in **UNTIL MORNING COMES,** LOVESWEPT #402. In this emotional story, Peggy captures the stark beauty of the Arizona desert and the fragile beauty of the love two very different people find together. In San Francisco he's known as Dr. Colter Gray, but in the land of his Apache ancestors, he's Gray Wolf. Reconciling the two aspects of his identity becomes a torment to Colter, but when he meets Jo Beth McGill, his life heads in a new direction. Jo Beth has brought her elderly parents along on her assignment to photograph the desert cacti. Concerned about her father's increasing senility, Jo Beth has vowed never to abandon her parents to the perils of old age. But when she meets Colter, she worries that she'll have to choose between them. When Colter appears on his stallion in the moonlight, ready to woo her with ancient Apache love rituals, Jo Beth trembles with excitement and gives herself up to the mysterious man in whose arms she finds her own security. This tender story deals with love on many levels and will leave you with a warm feeling in your heart.

In LOVESWEPT #403 by Linda Cajio, all it takes is **JUST ONE LOOK** for Remy St. Jacques to fall for the beguiling seductress Susan Kitteridge. Ordered to shadow the woman he believes to be a traitor, Remy comes to realize the lady who drives him to sweet obsession could not be what she seemed. Afraid of exposing those she loves to danger, Susan is caught up in the life of lies she'd live for so long. But she yearns to confess all to Remy the moment the bayou outlaw captures her lips with his. In her smooth, sophisticated style, Linda creates a winning love story you won't be able to put down. As an added treat, Linda brings back the lovable character of Lettice as her third and last granddaughter finds true happiness and love. Hint! Hint! This won't be the last you'll hear of Lettice, though. Stay tuned!

(continued)

With her debut book, **PERFECT MORNING,** published in April 1989, Marcia Evanick made quite a splash in the romance world. Next month Marcia returns to the LOVESWEPT lineup with **INDESCRIBABLY DELICIOUS,** LOVESWEPT #404. Marcia has a unique talent for blending the sensuality of a love story with the humorous trials and tribulations of single parenthood. When Dillon McKenzie follows a tantalizing scent to his neighbor's kitchen, he finds delicious temptation living next door! Elizabeth Lancaster is delighted that Dillon and his two sons have moved in; now her boy Aaron will have playmates. What she doesn't count on is becoming Dillon's playmate! He brings out all her hidden desires and makes her see there's so much more to life than just her son and the business she's built creating scrumptious cakes and candies. You'll be enthralled by these two genuine characters who must find a way to join their families as well as their dreams.

As promised, Tami Hoag returns with her second pot of pure gold in *The Rainbow Chasers* series, **KEEPING COMPANY,** LOVESWEPT #405. Alaina Montgomery just knew something would go wrong on her way to her friend Jayne's costume party dressed as a sexy comic-book princess. When her car konks out on a deserted stretch of road, she's more embarrassed by her costume than frightened of danger—until Dylan Harrison stops to help her. At first she believes he's an escaped lunatic, then he captivates her with his charm and incredible sex appeal—and Alaina actually learns to like him—even after he gets them arrested. A cool-headed realist, Alaina is unaccustomed to Dylan's care-free attitude toward life. So she surprises even herself when she accepts his silly proposal to "keep company" to curtail their matchmaking friends from interfering in their lives. Even more surprising is the way Dylan makes her feel, as if her mouth were made for long, slow kisses. Tami's flare for humor shines in this story of a reckless dreamer who teaches a lady lawyer to believe in magic.

In Judy Gill's **DESPERADO,** LOVESWEPT #406, hero Bruce Hagendorn carries the well-earned nickname of Stud. But there's much more to the former hockey star than his name implies—and he intends to convince his lovely neighbor, Mary Delaney, of that fact. After Mary saves him from a severe allergy attack that she had unintentionally caused, Bruce vows to coax his personal Florence Nightingale out to play. An intensely driven woman, Mary has set certain goals

(continued)

for herself that she's focused all her attention on attaining—doing so allows her to shut out the hurts from her past. But Bruce/Stud won't take no for an answer, and Mary finds herself caught under the spell of the most virile man she's ever met. She can't help wishing, though, that he'd tell her where he goes at night, what kind of business it is that he's so dedicated to. But Bruce knows once he tells Mary, he could lose her forever. This powerful story is sure to have an impact on the lives of many readers, as Judy deals with the ecstasy and the heartache true love can bring.

We're delighted as always to bring you another memorable romance from one of the ladies who's helped make LOVESWEPT so successful. Fayrene Preston's *SwanSea Place:* **DECEIT,** LOVESWEPT #407, is the *pièce de résistance* to a fabulous month of romantic reading awaiting you. Once again Fayrene transports you to Maine and the great estate of SwanSea Place, where Richard Zagen has come in search of Liana Marchall, the only woman he's ever loved. Richard has been haunted, tormented by memories of the legendary model he knows better as the heartless siren who'd left him to build her career in the arms of another. Liana knows only too well the desperate desire Richard is capable of making her feel. She's run once from the man who could give her astonishing pleasure and inflict shattering pain, but time has only deepened her hunger for him. Fayrene's characters create more elemental force than the waves crashing against the rocky coast. Let them sweep you up in their inferno of passion!

As always we invite you to write to us with your thoughts and comments. We hope your summer is off to a fabulous start! Sincerely,

Susann Brailey

Susann Brailey
Editor
LOVESWEPT
Bantam Books
666 Fifth Avenue
New York, NY 10103

FAN OF THE MONTH

Ricki L. Ebbs

I guess I started reading the LOVESWEPT series as soon as it hit the market. I had been looking for a different kind of romance novel, one that had humor, adventure, a little danger, some offbeat characters, and, of course, true love and a happy ending. When I read my first LOVESWEPT, I stopped looking.

Fayrene Preston, Kay Hooper, Iris Johansen, Joan Elliott Pickart, Sandra Brown, and Deborah Smith are some of my favorite authors. I love Kay Hooper's wonderful sense of humor. For pure sensuality, Sandra Brown's books are un-surpassed. Though their writing styles are different, Iris Johansen, Joan Elliott Pickart, and Fayrene Preston write humorous, touching, and wonderfully sentimental stories. Deborah Smith's books have a unique blend of adventure and romance, and she keeps bringing back those charac-ters I always wonder about at the end of the story. (I'm nosy about my friends' lives too.)

I'm single, with a terrific but demanding job as an adminis-trative assistant. When I get the chance, I always pick up a mystery or romance novel. I have taken some kidding from my family and friends for my favorite reading. My brother says I should have been Sherlock Holmes or Scarlett O'Hara. I don't care what they say. I may be one of the last roman-tics, but I think the world looks a little better with a slightly romantic tint, and LOVESWEPTs certainly help to keep it rosy.

THE DELANEY DYNASTY

THE SHAMROCK TRINITY

☐   21975   RAFE, THE MAVERICK
by Kay Hooper $2.95

☐   21976   YORK, THE RENEGADE
by Iris Johansen $2.95

☐   21977   BURKE, THE KINGPIN
by Fayrene Preston $2.95

THE DELANEYS OF KILLAROO

☐   21872   ADELAIDE, THE ENCHANTRESS
by Kay Hooper $2.75

☐   21873   MATILDA, THE ADVENTURESS
by Iris Johansen $2.75

☐   21874   SYDNEY, THE TEMPTRESS
by Fayrene Preston $2.75

THE DELANEYS: *The Untamed Years*

☐   21899   GOLDEN FLAMES *by Kay Hooper* $3.50

☐   21898   WILD SILVER *by Iris Johansen* $3.50

☐   21897   COPPER FIRE *by Fayrene Preston* $3.50

THE DELANEYS II

☐   21978   SATIN ICE *by Iris Johansen* $3.50

☐   21979   SILKEN THUNDER *by Fayrene Preston* $3.50

☐   21980   VELVET LIGHTNING *by Kay Hooper* $3.50
